Dear Reader

Can love overcome all obstacles?

That's the question Becky and Ewan have to find the answer to in this final book of my *Bride's Bay Surgery* series. Eight years ago they were deeply attracted to one another, but Becky realised that they wanted very different things out of life and married someone else. When she meets Ewan again she is shocked to discover that the old feelings she had for him are still very much alive. The fact that Ewan feels the same fills her with dread. She has nothing to offer Ewan these days.

Helping Becky and Ewan to find a way through their problems was a real joy, although I have to confess that I shed the odd tear when it looked as if they would never reach a solution! They are such a lovely couple that they deserved a happy ending, and I hope you will agree that I have given them that.

So...*do* I believe that love can overcome all obstacles? Yes, I do. I wouldn't be writing romance novels if I didn't believe it!

Love to you all

Jennifer

'Things just get on top of me at times, that's all.'

'It's only to be expected after everything you've been through.'

The kindness in his voice brought more tears to her eyes and she blinked them away. 'Perhaps. But I try to hold it together for Millie's sake.'

'I can understand that, but you can't be brave all the time. It won't do you any good in the long run.'

He touched her hand, his fingers lingering for just a moment before he turned to push the swing once more, but Becky felt a frisson of awareness race from her hand and travel through her entire body. It felt as though every cell was suddenly on fire, creating an immense amount of heat inside her. It had been ages since she had felt this way, she realised. Not since those first heady days when she had met Ewan at the hospital had a touch aroused her so swiftly, so completely.

THE REBEL
WHO LOVED HER

BY
JENNIFER TAYLOR

MILLS
BOON®

Published in Great Britain 2013
by Mills & Boon, an imprint of Harlequin (UK) Limited.
Large Print edition 2014
Harlequin (UK) Limited, Eton House,
18-24 Paradise Road, Richmond, Surrey, TW9 1SR

© 2013 Jennifer Taylor

ISBN: 978 0 263 23853 2

Printed and bound in Great Britain
by CPI Antony Rowe, Chippenham, Wiltshire

Jennifer Taylor lives in the north-west of England, in a small village surrounded by some really beautiful countryside. She has written for several different Mills & Boon® series in the past, but it wasn't until she read her first Medical Romance™ that she truly found her niche. She was so captivated by these heart-warming stories that she set out to write them herself! When she's not writing, or doing research for her latest book, Jennifer's hobbies include reading, gardening, travel, and chatting to friends both on and off-line. She is always delighted to hear from readers, so do visit her website at www.jennifer-taylor.com

Recent titles by the same author:

THE SON THAT CHANGED HIS LIFE†
THE FAMILY WHO MADE HIM WHOLE†
GINA'S LITTLE SECRET
SMALL TOWN MARRIAGE MIRACLE
THE MIDWIFE'S CHRISTMAS MIRACLE
THE DOCTOR'S BABY BOMBSHELL*
THE GP'S MEANT-TO-BE BRIDE*
MARRYING THE RUNAWAY BRIDE*
THE SURGEON'S FATHERHOOD SURPRISE**

†*Bride's Bay Surgery*
**Dalverston Weddings*
***Brides of Penhally Bay*

**These books are also available in eBook format
from www.millsandboon.co.uk**

Good friends are scarcer than hens' teeth
and I am very lucky to have some of
the very best friends possible.

So a huge thank you to Barbara, Charlotte and Ted,
Jeremy, and John.

Life wouldn't be half as much fun without you all.

CHAPTER ONE

'BECKY! HEY, BECKY…wait!'

Becky Williams stopped when she heard someone calling her name. Turning around, she peered at the faces of the other passengers gathered in the baggage hall of Heathrow Airport. The flight had been long and arduous despite the fact that her parents had insisted on upgrading her and Millie to business class. Twenty-plus hours non-stop from New Zealand would have been hard enough on her own, but it had been little short of gruelling with a small child in tow.

Becky sighed when Millie started to whimper. She cuddled her close, hoping it wouldn't be too long before their pushchair appeared on the carousel. At fourteen months, Millie was getting quite heavy and Becky's arms were aching from the long hours spent holding her as they had flown across the globe.

'I thought it was you!'

All of a sudden a man was standing in front of her and Becky jumped. She stared at him in confusion. He was tall, several inches taller than her own not inconsiderable height, in fact, with dark brown hair and the most wonderful deep blue eyes. Although his face wasn't classically handsome, there was something very appealing about those craggy features and the upward curve of his mouth that hinted at a well-developed sense of humour....

'Don't tell me you don't recognise me. I'm gutted!' He grinned at her, his face lighting up in a way that was all too familiar, and Becky gasped.

'Ewan! Is it really you?'

'It is indeed.' He gave her a quick hug, his strong arms closing around her for the briefest of moments before he drew back. His blue eyes sparkled with laughter as he stared down at her. 'Or at least I *think* it's me. After all those hours in the air I'm not sure if I'm actually here or not!'

He laughed, mercifully missing her reaction. Becky sucked in her breath as she took a firmer hold of Millie. She was tired, that was all, tired and stressed after the long hours spent travelling. It was little wonder that it had felt so good to have Ewan hold her but it didn't mean anything. She may have had a massive crush on Ewan MacLeod at one point but that was all in the past. An awful lot had happened since then.

The thought of what had happened in the past year was never far from her mind, but Becky pushed it aside, knowing that she couldn't cope with all the soul searching right then. The baggage carousel began to move and people stepped forward to look for their luggage. Becky spotted their pushchair and tried to force her way through the crowd but with Millie in her arms, it wasn't easy.

'Is that yours?' Ewan gently moved her aside when she nodded. Leaning over, he lifted the pushchair off the carousel and set it down in front of her. He quickly opened it so she could place Millie in the seat then crouched down before Becky could do so and fastened the safety harness, smiling at the little girl as he did so. 'There you go, poppet. You can have a little nap now.'

He ruffled Millie's honey-gold curls and Becky did her best to hide her surprise when Millie laughed. Normally, Millie was wary of strangers. Maybe it was all the upset of the past twelve months but Millie's usual response when she was approached by someone she didn't know was to cry. However, there was no sign of tears now, just the opposite, in fact.

Ewan straightened up and Becky hurriedly smoothed her face into a suitably noncommittal expression. Maybe Millie had responded unusually favourably but it meant no more than her own reaction had. They were both exhausted and the sooner they were home in Bride's Bay the better. She glanced at the carousel, willing her suitcase to appear. Cases were being claimed from all sides but she couldn't see any sign of her bag.

Ewan reached over and grabbed a battered old holdall and dropped it on the floor by his feet. 'That's mine sorted. There's just yours to come now. Shout out when you spot it.'

He seemed to have taken it for granted that he should help her and Becky wasn't sure what to do. It didn't seem fair to make use of him, especially not after the way they had parted all those years ago. The guilt that had become such a large part of her life of late rose up inside her and she shook her head.

'Don't worry about us, Ewan. We can manage. You've got your bag so you get on off home.'

'And leave you to struggle on your own?' His dark brows rose. 'I can just imagine what my mother would say if she found out. She'd have my guts for garters!'

Becky summoned a smile. 'I think you're a bit too old to worry what your mother will say.'

'True.' His smile faded and he looked at her with a seriousness that made a shiver pass through her. 'However, I'd never forgive myself if I abandoned you, Becky. Mum wrote and told me what had happened to Steve. I'm really sorry. Losing your husband like that must have been horrendous. You've had a really rough time and I'd like to help any way I can, even if it's only by seeing to your luggage.'

Becky felt a lump come to her throat when she heard genuine concern in his voice and looked away. She was afraid that she would do something silly if she wasn't careful, and cry. She had learned to hold back her tears in the past year for Millie's sake. It hadn't seemed fair to upset her daughter so what little crying she'd done had been done in private. Maybe it was tiredness or the fact that she'd been caught unawares by seeing Ewan again, but she knew it would take very little to make her break down.

'Thank you,' she said quietly. 'You're very kind.'

'It's my pleasure.' He touched her hand then turned towards the carousel, thankfully missing the start she gave.

Becky took a deep breath as she focused on the cases travelling along the conveyor belt. She *was* tired, so it was little wonder that she seemed to be overreacting. The fact that her pulse had started racing when Ewan had touched her wasn't an indication of anything else.

She finally spotted her case and pointed to it. 'That's my case—the red one with the yellow tag on it.'

'Okey-dokey.' Ewan elbowed his way through

the crowd and lifted the case off the belt with an ease that belied its weight. Setting it down on the floor, he looked at her. 'I take it that you're being met?'

'Yes.' Becky sighed. 'Mum and Dad insisted on coming to meet us. I tried to talk them out of it but they were adamant.'

'Of course they were.' Ewan frowned as he released the handle of her suitcase and turned it towards the exit. 'You've just flown right across the globe, Becky. Anyone would be tired after a journey like that—I know I am. Plus you've had the added stress of looking after your daughter. What's the point of making your life even more difficult by refusing to let your parents collect you?'

Becky bit her lip. What Ewan had said made sense but she still felt bad about her parents making the long drive from Devon. They had been through enough in the past year thanks to her and she was determined that she wasn't going to put them under any more pressure. Once again the thought that she might be making a mistake by returning to England rose to her mind.

She'd thought long and hard before she had made her decision but, in the end, she had accepted that she didn't have a choice. She needed to work to provide for herself and Millie, and the cost of full-time childcare would have been exorbitant. There simply wouldn't have been enough money left over each month to pay all the other bills. Her parents had not only offered her and Millie a home, but her mother had offered to look after Millie while Becky went out to work. Becky knew that she should be grateful for their kindness, and she was, but it wasn't easy to sacrifice her independence. She would be right back where she'd been eight years ago, living with her parents and dreaming about Ewan.

The thought slid into her mind so fast that she didn't have time to stop it. Becky shook her head, determined to dislodge it as she followed Ewan towards the exit. There was no chance of history repeating itself. Maybe she had fallen under Ewan's spell once upon a time but it was Steve she had married and Steve she had loved....

Hadn't she?

Becky felt her breath catch as her eyes rested

on Ewan's broad back. All of a sudden she wasn't sure what was true any more. Had she loved Steve, *really* loved him, or had he merely fitted her idea of the perfect husband? Steve had appeared so calm and dependable, so focused on what he wanted from life. They'd held similar views, shared the same objectives—marriage, a home and a family—that she had believed she had found her soulmate. Ewan, however, had been very, very different.

Ewan had been charming, funny, exciting, sexy—everything Steve hadn't. Although he'd had numerous girlfriends, he'd made no secret of the fact that he didn't plan on settling down. As he'd stated on many occasions there was a great big world waiting to be explored and he was going to do his level best to see as much of it as possible. Even though she had been deeply attracted to him, and had known he'd felt the same about her, Becky had realised it wouldn't work. They had wanted such different things out of life that any kind of relationship had been doomed from the outset.

In the end she had chosen to stay with Steve,

sure in her own mind that it was the right decision. Steve had offered her the security she'd wanted, the chance to create a marriage exactly like her parents'—stable and enduring. It was only now, looking back, that she found herself wondering if she had made the biggest mistake of her life. Who knew what might have happened if she had chosen Ewan?

Ewan could feel a knot of tension twisting his guts. He took a deep breath, forcing the oxygen through his lungs. Seeing Becky at Christchurch Airport had been a shock admittedly, but he'd had hours to get over it. As he had sat in the cramped confines of the aircraft, he had, quite deliberately, gone over everything that had happened eight years ago.

He'd been doing his rotations and Becky had been in her final year, training as a nurse, when they had met at the hospital where they were both seconded. Although they both came from the Bride's Bay area, he was a few years older than her so she'd not been part of his set. It had been a while since he'd seen her, in fact, and

Ewan had been surprised by how attractive she was. Not only was she extremely pretty but she had a lively and engaging mind.

He'd got into the habit of stopping by the ward she was on, timing his visits to coincide with her breaks. They'd chatted about this and that over coffee, but each knew the conversation was merely a cover for their real feelings. If he was attracted to her then it was obvious that Becky felt the same about him. Although he knew that she was seeing someone—a definite no-no in his book as he made a point of never encroaching on another man's territory—he asked her out and she accepted.

They went for dinner at a little bistro down by the river recommended by one of his friends. Candlelight, soft music, discreetly attentive waiters—it was so self-consciously *romantic* that it would have been laughable if Ewan hadn't been mortified in case Becky thought he was trying to seduce her. However, when he apologised, she simply laughed. And it was then that he realised he could very easily fall in love with her.

He drove her home afterwards with his head

in a spin. He had always ruled out the possibility of falling in love just yet. He wanted to see something of the world before he settled down and making a commitment like that would make that impossible. However, meeting Becky had changed everything; he was no longer certain what he wanted any more. And when he kissed her, right there in the street, he was less certain than ever. Maybe he had found something even more wonderful than anything the world had to offer?

In other circumstances he might have asked her if he could spend the night with her but what had happened was just too profound. He drove himself home in a state of turmoil, aware that he needed to decide what he was going to do. However, before he could work it out, Becky came to see him. She told him that she and Steve were getting engaged and that in the circumstances she didn't think they should see each other again. Whilst Ewan was stunned by the announcement, he was also relieved. Now he could carry on with his plans, do everything he wanted to do. There was nothing and no one to hold him back, although if Becky hadn't called a halt, he wasn't sure if he could have done so…

Ewan cursed under his breath as they reached the arrivals hall. He was acting like an idiot by thinking about all that. It was over and done with and they had both moved on. Turning, he smiled at Becky, seeing the dark circles that exhaustion had painted under her eyes. His hands clenched because it was all he could do not to reach out and smooth them away.

'Where did your parents say they'd meet you?'

'They said they'd be waiting when I came through Customs…' She broke off, a smile lighting her face. 'There they are!'

Ewan turned, glad of the excuse not to look at her. When she smiled like that she looked like the old Becky, the one he had found so beguiling, and it wasn't easy to reconcile the mix of emotions that thought aroused. There had been umpteen women in his life since Becky. Admittedly, none of them had made much of an impression on him, but he hadn't wanted them to. He'd been happy to play the field and enjoy his life as a bachelor. Maybe he had decided it was time he settled down, but he wasn't in a rush. He would wait until he found the right woman…

If he hadn't found her already.

Ewan felt alarm scud through him. Was Becky that woman? Was it possible that he was still attracted to her? He didn't want to believe it but he couldn't pretend that he didn't feel anything. Maybe it was only sympathy because of what she'd been through, but, there again, maybe it was something more.

He groaned. Once again it felt as though all his plans were up in the air. And once again it was all down to Becky!

CHAPTER TWO

'DARLING, IT'S SO wonderful to see you!'

Becky smiled as her mother enveloped her in a hug. She hugged her back, surprised by the feeling of relief that swept over her. Maybe she did have reservations about coming back to England, but she couldn't deny that it was good to know she wasn't on her own anymore. She kissed her mother's cheek then turned to her father.

'Hello, Dad. How are you?'

'All the better for seeing you, sweetheart.' Simon Harper gave her a bear hug then bent down and chucked Millie under the chin. 'And for seeing you, too, poppet.'

Becky felt a lump come to her throat when she saw tears in his eyes. Her parents had been marvellous and she knew that she wouldn't have coped without their support. No matter how difficult it was, she was going to make sure their new living arrangements worked for all of them. Perhaps it would be like stepping back in time, but that didn't necessarily mean it was a bad thing. A lot of good things had happened in the past, like her friendship with Ewan.

Heat rushed through her as she glanced at him. He was standing to one side, obviously giving them the chance to say their hellos in private. It was so typically considerate of him that Becky's heartstrings twanged. Despite his playboy image, Ewan had always been incredibly thoughtful. It was one of the reasons why she'd been attracted to him, that plus the fact that he'd been so exciting and sexy, of course. She had never felt bored when she was with Ewan but wonderfully, vibrantly alive.

She blanked out the thought as she turned to her mother again. She wouldn't allow herself to be seduced by memories. She'd had her fill of relationships and she didn't intend to make the mistake of getting involved again. 'Ewan very kindly helped me with my luggage.'

'Ewan?' Ros Harper repeated uncertainly as she glanced at him. Her face suddenly cleared and she smiled in delight. 'Ewan! What a wonderful surprise.'

'It's good to see you too, Mrs Harper.' Ewan stepped forward and shook hands with Ros then turned to Simon. 'And you, too, sir.'

Simon smiled warmly as he shook the younger man's hand. 'Make that Simon, eh? I heard via the grapevine that you were coming back to England, although I thought you'd been working in Australia, not New Zealand.'

'I was,' Ewan agreed. 'I did a twelve-month stint at a hospital in Sydney.' He shrugged. 'I did consider staying on there but in the end the lure of home was too strong. I popped over to New Zealand on my way back to visit my sister. Shona's third child is due any day and I was hoping it would arrive while I was there, but no such luck.'

'Another grandchild for your parents!' Ros exclaimed. 'How many is that now?'

'Eight...or is it nine?' Ewan grinned. 'I've lost track. We MacLeods tend to be highly productive in the baby-making department.'

Everyone laughed at the comment, Becky included, although there was a hollow ache inside her. She bent down, tucking a lightweight blanket around Millie so that nobody would notice how much it hurt. She still found it hard to accept that she would never have another child. She loved children and had planned to have at least four, but the accident that had cost Steve his life had robbed her of that chance. She stood up, feeling her heart lurch when she caught Ewan's eyes and saw the concern they held. Surely, he hadn't realised something was wrong?

'Right, let's get you two home.'

Her father's voice broke into her thoughts. Becky quickly settled her bag on her shoulder then took a deep breath before turning to Ewan. Maybe he did suspect that something wasn't right but that was all it would ever be—a suspicion. She wasn't going to tell Ewan the truth about the accident, wasn't going to tell anyone, in fact. It was hard enough having to live with the guilt without everyone knowing what she had done.

'Thank you again for all your help, Ewan. It really was kind of you.'

'My pleasure.'

He smiled but his deep blue eyes were searching as they rested on her. Becky shifted uncom-
fortably. Maybe she didn't plan on telling people
the truth but if anyone could get it out of her, it
would be Ewan. She had told Ewan things that
she'd told no one else, not even Steve. Definitely
not Steve.

He looked away and she breathed a sigh of relief, which was short-lived when she heard her
father ask him if he wanted a lift. Although she
knew it was selfish, she couldn't face the thought
of having to travel all the way back to Devon
with Ewan in the car in her present frame of
mind.

'Thank you, but I'm staying in London with
my brother until I can sort out my accommoda-
tion. Ryan and I plan to down a few beers and
catch up on what's been happening.' He laughed.
'Always assuming I manage to stay awake long
enough, of course!'

He smiled at them, his gaze lingering a fraction longer on Becky, but she didn't respond.
Maybe he would think she was being churl-

ish but it was better than allowing herself to be drawn into making a confession. When he bade them farewell, she didn't make a fuss, certainly didn't make any attempt to arrange to see him again. Meeting him like this had been a chance encounter. It wasn't an excuse to resume their former relationship.

Becky knew she was doing the right thing, yet it didn't explain the sense of loss she felt as she watched him wending his way through the crowd. Even though she knew it was foolish, she was going to miss him.

Ewan took a taxi to his brother's flat and let himself in, using the key Ryan had left with a neighbour. He dumped his bag on the living room floor and flopped down onto a chair with a sigh that stemmed partly from weariness but mainly from frustration. What was wrong with Becky? Why had she behaved so warily towards him?

Closing his eyes, he tried to conjure up her image, surprised by how easy it was. He'd not thought about her in ages and yet—hey, presto!—there she was in his head: honey-gold hair, hazel eyes, that pert little nose. She had changed, of course, but she was still incredibly pretty. Although she was a shade too thin in his opinion, she had a very feminine figure with curves in all the right places....

He groaned as his body responded with predictable enthusiasm to that thought. He might be bone-tired but his libido was in fine fettle! Not that it should be a surprise because Becky had always had this effect on him. In fact, he couldn't think of a single woman he'd dated in the past eight years who had aroused him the way Becky had done.

The thought was too near the knuckle. Ewan got up and went into the kitchen. Ryan had told him to make himself at home so he took him at his word as he set to and made himself a fry-up. Eggs, bacon, sausages—the plate was heaving by the time he finished. He sat down at the table and tucked in, but after a couple of mouthfuls was forced to admit defeat. He didn't want food. He wanted answers. He wanted to know what was wrong with Becky and he wouldn't rest until he found out, although he refused to delve too deeply into the reason why. Suffice it to say that Becky had meant a lot to him at one point. Even though that was all in the past, he hoped they could be friends.

He got up and scraped the uneaten food into the bin, trying to ignore the mocking little voice in his head. Friendship was all he wanted from her. Nothing more!

It was several days before Becky got over her jet-lag. Fortunately, Millie didn't seem to be affected by it and soon settled down in their new home. Her parents had had her old room redecorated so it felt less like stepping back in time than it could have done. They'd also turned her brother's room into a bright and cheerful nursery, complete with lots of colourful posters of Millie's favourite cartoon characters.

Becky could tell they'd gone to a great deal of trouble to make her and Millie feel welcome and she was grateful, but it still felt odd to be living under their roof again. She made up her mind that she would find a place of her own as soon as she could, and that meant finding a job. Although she scoured the local papers each day, there were very few jobs available. As a highly qualified nurse practitioner, she had a lot to offer, but cutbacks in the health service meant there were few posts being advertised. All she could hope was that something would turn up eventually.

She was washing the breakfast dishes a week after she'd returned when her father poked his head round the kitchen door. Millie was helping her and the floor was awash with soap suds. 'Mind you don't slip,' she warned him. 'This little lady gets as much water on the floor as she gets on the dishes.'

'I wonder who she takes after,' Simon said, drolly. He stepped over the puddles and dropped a kiss on his granddaughter's head. 'You are doing a wonderful job helping Mummy, poppet.'

Millie smiled beatifically as she beat her small hands up and down in the water and Becky groaned. 'It'll be like Noah's flood in here soon. We'll need our very own ark!'

Simon laughed. 'It's only water, sweetheart. It

will soon mop up. Anyway, seeing as Millie is happily occupied, can I have a word?'

'Of course.' Becky dried her hands on a towel, wondering what he wanted to speak to her about. 'Nothing's wrong, is there?'

'No, no, not at all,' Simon assured her. 'It's just that I have a proposition for you but before I tell you what it is, I want you to promise me that you'll say no if you don't like the idea.'

'That sounds very mysterious,' Becky said, laughing.

Simon smiled. 'I suppose it does. It's just that I don't want you to feel that you're under any sort of...well, obligation.'

'Curiouser and curiouser. Come on, Dad, tell me what's going on.'

'All right. You know that Brenda Roberts took over as practice nurse at the surgery when Emily left to get married?'

'Yes. Brenda came out of retirement so she could help you.'

'That's right.' Simon sighed. 'I was really grateful to her, too. Although we had plenty of interest when we advertised the post, we didn't find anyone who we felt would fit in.'

'It's difficult to find the right person,' Becky observed.

'Exactly. Anyway, Brenda's just informed me that she would like to leave at the end of the month. Apparently, her husband, Fred, is taking early retirement and they've decided to go and live in their apartment in Spain.'

'What a shame!' Becky exclaimed. 'Not for Brenda and Fred of course, but it's going to make life difficult for you and the rest of the team.'

'It is. It will mean us having to advertise again and that will take time. That's why I was wondering if you'd consider helping out?'

'You want me to cover until you find someone?'

'Yes. Or, better still, maybe consider taking the job on a permanent basis,' Simon said quietly. 'With all the changes we're having to make now that we've been awarded health centre status, I need staff I can rely on. You fit the bill perfectly, darling, although I'll understand if you feel it's too much, living and working with your father.'

'I'd never thought about it,' Becky said slowly. 'But it does make sense. I mean, I need a job and if I'm working here at the surgery then I'll be on hand for Millie. I have to admit that I was worried about leaving her for long stretches, even if she was with Mum.'

'So you'll think about it?' Simon said hopefully.

Becky smiled. 'There's nothing to think about. I'd be delighted to take the job if you think I'm suitable.'

'Great!' Simon gave her a hug then glanced at his watch. He grimaced. 'I know this is a bit of cheek, but is there any chance that you could start right away? We're overrun with patients needing BP checks this morning and it would really help to take the pressure off us if you would give Brenda a hand.'

'Slave driver!' Becky laughed. 'Of course I can start immediately, so long as Mum will look after Millie.'

'Oh, there's no problem about that. Your mother is longing to have this little one all to herself for a couple of hours,' Simon assured her. 'I'll just let her know what's happening.'

Becky cleared up after her father left, feeling her spirits lift when it struck her that she'd taken her first step towards regaining her independence. Once she was earning regular money, she could look for a place of her own, somewhere she could turn into a proper home for her and Millie. Millie needed stability after all the recent upsets and Becky was determined she was going to give her that.

A shadow darkened her face as she lifted the little girl down from the chair and dried her hands. What had Steve said during their last fateful conversation, that he wished they'd never had a child? Her mouth compressed. No way was Millie ever going to find out that her father had wished she hadn't been born! It had been a terrible thing to say even in the heat of anger. She couldn't imagine Ewan even thinking such a thing, let alone saying it.

She sighed as once again she found herself thinking about Ewan. Although she had tried to blot out all thoughts of him, she hadn't succeeded. Their chance encounter had affected her far more than it should have done and she could only thank her lucky stars that it was unlikely they would meet again. Their paths certainly wouldn't cross when Ewan was working in London and she was living and working here.

'Mrs Rose? I'm Ewan MacLeod, one of the registrars. I believe you took a bit of a tumble this morning.'

Ewan smiled at the elderly lady lying on the bed. It was midday and he hadn't stopped since he'd arrived at six that morning. The emergency department of Pinscombe General Hospital was a very busy place. It served the communities of three major towns plus a number of smaller ones like Bride's Bay.

His heart gave that all-too-familiar jolt it had started doing every time Bride's Bay was mentioned, and he swallowed a sigh. He really was a sad case if the mere mention of the place where Becky lived had this effect on him. Drawing up a chair, he sat down beside the bed. It was time to concentrate on his patient.

'Can you tell me what happened, Mrs Rose?'

'It was so silly, really,' the old lady replied. 'I was carrying my washing out to peg it on the line when I tripped over Mog.'

'Mog? Who's that, then? Your dog?'

'No, my cat, of course,' Edith Rose said sharply, treating him to a frosty glare.

Ewan grimaced. 'My mistake. Sorry.' He frowned. 'But why on earth did you call your cat Mog? I thought moggies were mice.'

'Hmm, it all depends which part of the country you come from,' Mrs Rose informed him tartly. 'Where I come from, young man, a moggy is a cat.'

'I stand corrected.' Ewan laughed, pleased to see that there was nothing wrong with her mental faculties. He had a feeling that Mrs Rose wouldn't appreciate the usual questions used to determine an elderly patient's mental prowess, such as the date and the name of the current prime minister. He put a tick in the relevant box on the patient's history and heard the old lady sniff.

'Convinced you that I'm compos mentis, have I?'

'Absolutely.' Ewan put the clipboard down and

folded his arms. 'There's nothing wrong with your mind, Mrs Rose.'

'I wish you'd tell that to my son. He seems to think I'm going gaga. No doubt he'll try to use this as an excuse to put me into a nursing home.'

Ewan frowned when he heard the tremor in the old lady's voice. 'I take it that it isn't what you want?'

'Certainly not. I've lived on my own for almost forty years now since my husband died. I couldn't bear the thought of having to live with a group of strangers.'

'There's no reason why you should have to leave your home because of this accident,' Ewan assured her. He picked up the tablet computer and showed her the X-ray she'd had done on admission. 'There's no sign of a fracture. Granted, your leg is badly bruised and the cut will need dressing to make sure it heals properly, but you'll be back on your feet in no time.'

'Are you sure?' Relief washed over the old lady's face when he nodded. 'Thank heavens. Geoffrey has been going on and on about me moving into a home and I was sure this would be the excuse he needed to have me admitted.'

Ewan shook his head. 'No. So long as you feel that you can manage on your own, that's fine. And even if you do have problems, there's help available. Your GP should be able to put you in touch with social services and they can assess the level of help you need.'

'That's a weight off my mind, I can tell you.' Edith Rose smiled at him. 'Thank you, young man. You've made an old lady very happy.'

'Good.' Ewan laughed as he stood up. 'I'm just going to phone your GP and let him know what's happened. As I said, your leg will need dressing so we need to arrange for it to be done at the surgery.'

'Old flesh doesn't heal as fast as young does,' Mrs Rose observed wryly and he grinned.

'I'm afraid not.'

He went to the desk to make the call, unsurprised to discover that Mrs Rose was registered with Bride's Bay Surgery. A lot of the people he'd seen since he'd started at Pinscombe General had been registered with the practice, which meant it must be a very busy place to work. He asked to speak to the practice nurse when the receptionist answered, shaking his head when one of the nurses came over to see if he could look at a patient for her.

'I'm tied up at the moment,' he began then stopped when a voice came over the line, a voice that was all too familiar.

'Sister Williams speaking. How may I help you?'

Ewan turned to face the wall, not wanting anything to distract him. The one thing he had never anticipated was that Becky would answer his call. He took a deep breath, deliberately ironing all trace of emotion from his voice. Maybe it did feel as though his head was being whirled around inside a washing machine on the spin cycle but he wasn't going to let Becky know that.

'Becky, it's Ewan MacLeod.' He gave a short laugh, praying that it sounded less forced to her than it did to him. 'This is a surprise. Again!'

CHAPTER THREE

'EWAN!'

Becky felt shock race through her when she recognised Ewan's voice. It was all she could do to concentrate as he continued in the same teasing tone.

'Of all the surgeries in all the world…. I had no idea you were working there.'

'I…um…it came as a surprise to me too, actually.' She finally managed to gather her addled wits, relieved to hear that she sounded almost normal. Maybe it had been a surprise to hear Ewan's voice but did it really explain why it had sent her into such a spin? She blanked out the thought, not wanting to set off down a route that was guaranteed to lead to more questions. 'Dad needed a practice nurse for the surgery and asked me if I'd consider taking the job, and I agreed.'

'Sounds ideal to me. Not only are you able to earn your living but you're on hand if Millie needs you.'

'Exactly,' Becky agreed, wondering how he always managed to hit on the salient point. Ewan possessed the rare ability to cut through all the dross and see the bigger picture. It was something else she had admired about him, she realised, his ability to get to the heart of a matter with so little fuss. Steve had been the exact opposite, sadly. He'd got so caught up in the details that he had often failed to appreciate the real crux of an issue. Whenever that had happened, he had blamed everyone else, too, rather than himself. It was one of the things she had disliked most about him, in fact.

The thought made her feel incredibly guilty. It didn't seem right that she should compare the two men, especially when she had found her late husband lacking. She hurried on, wanting to get the conversation onto a more solid footing. 'Anyway, I take it that this isn't a social call?'

'No. I have one of your patients with me, a Mrs Edith Rose.' Ewan was all business as he explained what had happened. 'The cut on her leg is quite deep and it will need dressing. I was hoping I could arrange for her to be seen at the surgery.'

'Of course.' Becky opened the diary, relieved to turn her attention to other matters. Ewan was Ewan and Steve had been Steve; she mustn't make the mistake of weighing one against the other. 'I'll book her in for Wednesday morning at eleven. If the dressing's only been done today, it would be better not to disturb it, although tell her to contact me if she has any problems, won't you?'

'I shall. She's a feisty old lady, very alert and determined, although she does seem worried that her son may try to use the accident as an excuse to have her admitted to a nursing home.'

'I see.' Becky frowned. 'You don't believe that's necessary, obviously.'

'Definitely not,' he said firmly. 'In my opinion, Mrs Rose is more than capable of looking after herself, although perhaps she could do with a bit of help.'

'Would you like me to have word with her

about what social services can offer?' Becky suggested.

'Are you a mind reader? That's exactly what I was going to ask you to do!'

Becky felt her breath catch when she heard him laugh. He really did have the most attractive laugh, she thought, so soft and deep and so very, very sexy. She took a quick breath, forcing some much-needed air into her lungs. 'Great minds think alike, or so they say?'

'They certainly do.'

There it was again, that delicious, toe-tingling rumble coming down the line, and Becky's lungs went into spasm once more. She was glad that Ewan didn't seem to expect a reply as he explained that he would fax through a copy of Mrs Rose's notes. By the time he'd finished, she was able to speak again, although she kept it brief, wary of pushing things too far.

'I'll make sure the information is entered on her file.'

'Thanks. Right, I won't keep you any longer. Good to speak to you, Becky. Maybe we'll run into one another again at some point.'

'Maybe.'

Becky hung up then went to the window, needing a few minutes to herself before she called in her next patient. So Ewan wasn't working in London as she'd thought. He was right here in Devon, just a few miles away. Even though it shouldn't make a scrap of difference, she knew that it did. Did she want to see him again? If anyone had suggested it a week ago, her answer would have been a resounding no, but she was no longer sure. Talking to Ewan had aroused feelings inside her she had never expected to feel again after what had happened with Steve.

Discovering that Steve had had an affair with one of his colleagues had turned her off sex. Even though she had tried to overcome her distaste and make a go of their marriage for Millie's sake, making love had become a penance rather than a pleasure. The fact that Steve had used it to excuse his own behaviour had only made matters worse. He'd called her frigid, told her that it was little wonder he'd had to seek comfort in another woman's arms. Although Becky had known it wasn't true, part of her had wondered if she was to blame in some way. Now, after talking to Ewan, she realised how unjust the accusation had been.

She wasn't frigid—far from it! She could and did respond to a man. However, the fact that it was Ewan who pushed all the right buttons was what worried her. Ewan wasn't interested in settling down. He enjoyed playing the field and one woman would never be enough for him, not that she was in the market for another relationship. She had tried her best to make her marriage work and failed, and she wasn't going to put herself through that heartache again, especially when there was even less chance now of a relationship working. Maybe Ewan was happily single at the moment but the time might come when he decided to settle down and start a family, and a family was the one thing she couldn't give him or any other man.

She sighed. It would be far better if she steered well clear of Ewan in future.

Ewan found it impossible to stop thinking about Becky. At odd moments throughout the week, thoughts of her would pop into his head. He couldn't rid himself of the thought that there was something troubling her and it only served to pique his interest even more. When his mother phoned and invited him to lunch on Sunday, he found himself agreeing even though he had planned to start redecorating the flat he was renting. The previous tenant had had a penchant for red and after a couple of weeks of waking up to pulsating scarlet walls, he desperately needed to do something about it. However, the décor could wait. Finding out what was worrying Becky seemed far more important.

He set off early on Sunday morning and made good time. It was the beginning of April and the main bulk of tourists hadn't arrived yet so the roads were clear. His parents lived in Denton's Cove but he bypassed the turning to their house and headed into Bride's Bay. It was just gone ten when he drew up outside the surgery, which was attached to Becky's parents' home, and he frowned when he saw all the building work that had been taking place. He'd heard that the practice had been awarded health centre status and it was obvious that a lot of changes were being made.

He made his way to the back door and lifted his hand to knock when he heard voices coming from the garden. Turning, he peered over the hedge and felt his heart lift when he saw Becky. She was pushing Millie on a pint-sized swing attached to a bough of the old apple tree. She was wearing jeans and a white sweater, her honey-gold hair pulled up into a ponytail. She looked so young and so lovely that Ewan felt his senses swim. Eight years may have passed but he was still attracted to her. It was only when Millie let out a shriek of laughter that he pulled himself together.

'It sounds as though you two are having fun,' he called, adopting a deliberately upbeat tone. He wasn't going to make the mistake of harking back to the past. Becky had chosen Steve and it had been the right decision for all of them. Maybe he would like to help her if he could but it was purely out of friendship. He wasn't planning to get back with her, not that Becky would be interested even if he was.

'Ewan!'

Ewan heard the dismay in her voice and grimaced. It was obvious that his arrival was less of a pleasant surprise than it could have been. He summoned a smile, not wanting her to suspect how much the idea stung. 'I thought I'd pop in to see how you were doing. I'm having lunch with my parents so I was heading this way.'

'Oh, I see.'

She dredged up a smile but it was such a poor effort that Ewan found himself wishing he hadn't bothered. Even if there was something troubling her, why would she choose to tell him?

'I should have phoned first.' He shrugged dismissively. Although he wasn't vain, most of the women he knew would have been more than happy to have him turn up on their doorsteps unannounced. 'I've been working in Australia for too long. I'd forgotten how much more formal life is here in England. Sorry.'

'It's fine, really. I…erm…it's nice to see you.'

Ewan's teeth snapped together. *Nice!* Quite frankly, she couldn't have said anything more guaranteed to offend him. The first prickle of anger ran through his veins and he smiled sardonically. 'There's no need to be polite, Becky. I can tell you're not exactly overjoyed to see me. Not to worry, I'm not stopping. Enjoy your day.'

He headed back up the path, his temper hovering just below boiling point. So Becky wasn't interested in seeing him; so what? It wasn't going to make any difference to his life.

'Ewan, wait!'

Ewan stopped reluctantly. He turned around, feeling his heart jolt when he saw her hurrying after him. She was carrying Millie in her arms and the picture they made was one he knew would stay with him for a long time to come. His pulse was racing when Becky came to a halt in front of him, the blood pounding through his veins in a way that made him feel both dizzy and yet wonderfully clear-headed.

This was what he wanted from life, he realised with sudden, startling clarity. He didn't need riches to be happy or professional acclaim. He just wanted someone to love and their child, and he would have everything he could possibly desire. The only thing wrong with the scenario was that it was Becky who featured in it, Becky who had made it abundantly clear that she didn't want anything to do with him!

Becky could feel herself trembling as she put Millie down. Even though she knew she was probably making a mistake, she couldn't let Ewan leave like this. He had come with the express intention of checking she was all right and all she'd done was throw his kindness back in his face.

'Don't go,' she said, her voice catching. 'I know I wasn't exactly welcoming, but please don't leave like this.'

'There's no point my staying if you don't want me here.' His tone was cool and she shivered. Ewan sighed softly. 'It's all right, Becky. I understand, really I do.'

'Do you?' It was impossible to keep the anxiety out of her voice and he grimaced.

'Yes. You're worried in case I want to pick up where we left off.' He didn't give her chance to reply as he continued flatly. 'Well, there's no need. That's all in the past and I just thought it would be good if we could be friends.'

'Friends?' she echoed uncertainly. Was he right? Was she worried in case he tried to res- urrect their relationship, or was it more compli- cated than that?

'Yes.' He smiled. 'I could be wrong, but I've a feeling you could do with a friend right now.'

Becky felt a surge of emotion well up inside her when she heard the sympathy in his voice. She swallowed hard, desperately trying to hold back her tears. Ewan obviously realised her pre- dicament because he bent down and smiled at Millie.

'How about another go on the swing, poppet?'

Becky watched as he led Millie back into the garden. How had he known that she didn't want Millie to see her crying? she wondered. He had accused her of being a mind-reader the other day, but he appeared to be equally skilled in the art.

It was a worrying thought in view of the fact that there was a lot she didn't want him to know. Becky took her time, wanting to be sure that she had herself under control before she went to join him and Millie. The little girl was having the time of her life, kicking her legs up and down as Ewan pushed the swing.

''Gain! 'Gain!' she shouted each time the swing slowed down.

'That's high enough, sweetie. We don't want you flying right up into the sky, do we?' Ewan said, laughing. He glanced at Becky and raised his brows. 'All right?'

'Fine.' She shrugged, embarrassed about what had happened. Normally, she kept a rein on her emotions but she didn't seem able to do that when Ewan was around. 'Things just get on top of me at times, that's all.'

'It's only to be expected after everything you've been through.'

The kindness in his voice brought more tears to her eyes and she blinked them away. 'Perhaps. But I try to hold it together for Millie's sake.'

'I can understand that, but you can't be brave all the time. It won't do you any good in the long run.'

He touched her hand, his fingers lingering for just a moment before he turned to push the swing once more, but Becky felt a frisson of awareness race from her hand and travel through her entire body. It felt as though every cell was suddenly on fire, creating an immense amount of heat inside her. It had been ages since she had felt this way, she realised. Not since those first heady days when she had met Ewan at the hospital had a touch aroused her so swiftly, so completely. She had never felt this way with Steve, not even when they had made love.

The thought was too unsettling to deal with. Becky summoned a smile, refusing to dwell on it. 'Do you fancy a cup of coffee?'

'I'd love one, but don't go to any trouble on my account,' Ewan said flatly. 'I didn't mean to intrude, Becky. I just wanted to check you were all right.'

'I know.' She looked into his eyes, feeling warmth envelop her again when she saw the concern they held. Despite the less than effusive reception he'd received, it was obvious that Ewan genuinely cared about her. She sighed, knowing that she owed him an apology. 'I really do appreciate you coming here, Ewan, even if it didn't seem like it.'

'It doesn't matter. So long as you're all right, that's the main thing.'

He smiled at her, his face breaking into a heart-melting smile, and Becky's heart did what was expected and melted. She turned away, afraid that if she didn't put some distance between them she would do something really stupid. Hurrying into the kitchen, she filled the kettle, her mind racing. Tempting though it was, it wouldn't be fair to pour out the whole story to Ewan and expect him to absolve her of any guilt. Maybe he wanted them to be friends, but how would he feel if he found out the truth about the accident and her part in it? Would he still want to be her friend then?

Pain lanced her heart as she watched him pushing the swing. She wouldn't blame him if he didn't want anything to do with her when he found out that she was responsible for Steve's death.

CHAPTER FOUR

'THAT'S GREAT. Thank you.'

Ewan spooned sugar into the mug of coffee that Becky had placed in front of him, wondering what on earth he was doing. What was the point of dragging this out when it was obvious that she had mixed feelings about him being here? He should have taken his leave when he'd had the chance, once he was sure she was all right.

He sighed as he watched her carry Millie into the house for her morning nap. Seeing Becky cry like that had been so damned hard. He had ached to take her in his arms and comfort her, but what comfort could he have offered when she was grieving for the man she loved? His heart spasmed with a pain that surprised him. It shouldn't matter how Becky felt about her late husband, but he'd be lying if he said that he didn't care.

'She went out like a light. She'll probably sleep till lunchtime by the look of her.'

Becky came back and sat down. Ewan summoned a smile, determined that he wasn't going to let her know how ambivalent he felt. Maybe he was still attracted to her but that was all it was; he'd get over it. 'She seems happy enough, I must say. I take it that she's adapted to living here.'

'She has.'

Becky picked up her mug and blew gently on her coffee to cool it. Ewan looked away when he felt his stomach muscles clench. The sight of her beautiful lips puckering that way was playing havoc with his self-control. He had to force himself to concentrate as she continued in a no-nonsense tone that immediately demolished any half-baked ideas he'd been harbouring about her doing it deliberately. Becky definitely wasn't trying to be provocative!

'I was really worried that the move would unsettle her but Millie's taken it in her stride. She seems really happy living here with my parents.'

'It must be a relief,' Ewan observed, doing his best to match her tone. He had to accept that Becky wasn't interested in him *that* way. Maybe she had been interested once but it was a long time ago.

'It is.' She took a sip of coffee then put the mug down with a sigh. 'Although it wasn't just Millie I was worried about, if I'm honest. I wasn't sure if moving back here was the right thing for me either.'

'Because it was a wrench to leave the life you and Steve had created for yourselves?' he suggested, although it felt a little like rubbing salt into a wound. However, he couldn't ignore the fact that she had been married even if he wanted to.

'It was more the thought of having to move back in with my parents, actually,' she admitted, then flushed when he looked at her in surprise.

'Really?' Ewan found it impossible to keep the astonishment out of his voice.

'Yes, really.' Her tone was defensive. 'Steve

and I hadn't lived in Christchurch for very long. We moved around quite a bit so that Steve could further his career.' She shrugged. 'I expect that's why it didn't seem such a wrench to leave—I hadn't had time to put down any roots.'

'I see.' It made sense, yet Ewan had a feeling that it wasn't the real explanation. He frowned as he weighed up what he'd heard. Had Becky's marriage not been as happy as he'd thought, or was he merely putting his own interpretation on what she'd said? He realised that he needed to find out, although he wasn't prepared to examine his reasons too closely. Suffice it to say that he needed to know all he could if he was to help her.

'So you moved to Christchurch because Steve got a job there?'

'That's right. I would have preferred to stay in the country for Millie's sake, but Steve was offered a consultant's post so we moved to the city. He didn't want to be too far from the hospital in case he was called in after hours,' she added hastily.

'I thought he worked in orthopaedics,' Ewan

said, frowning. In his experience it was rare for a consultant in that field to be called into work. Normally, one of the registrars would be expected to cover, unless it was some sort of life-threatening emergency, and they didn't happen very often.

'That's right.' She took another sip of her coffee and he sensed that she was playing for time. 'Steve was…well, he was very committed. He never minded being called back into work.'

'Highly commendable,' Ewan observed, wondering why he didn't believe her. Why on earth would Becky make such a claim if it weren't true? After all, it didn't matter to him how Steve had conducted his life. However, the fact that she had felt it necessary to lie piqued his interest. 'Did he get called in a lot?'

'Quite a bit.' She grimaced. 'You know what it's like—something crops up and the staff don't want to take responsibility so they call in the boss.'

It was so far removed from his own experiences that Ewan was stuck for an answer. Mercifully, he was saved from having to reply when

Becky's parents appeared. They had another couple with them plus a little boy, slightly older than Millie, and they greeted him in delight.

'Ewan! How lovely to see you.' Ros kissed him on the cheek. 'Becky didn't mention you were coming. I wish she had done. Simon and I wouldn't have gone for our weekly constitutional if we'd known you were planning to visit. It would have been the perfect excuse to enjoy a lazy Sunday morning!'

Ewan laughed as he stood up. 'Becky had no idea, I'm afraid. I'm having lunch with my parents so I decided to drop in on my way over there.'

'Well, I'm very glad that you did.' Ros turned to the other couple. 'You won't have met Ewan. His family live in Denton's Cove so he and Becky have known each other for years. He's a doctor too, although he's been working overseas for the past few years. Ewan, I'd like you to meet Tom and Hannah. They both work at the surgery. Oh, and this little fellow is Charlie.'

'Good to meet you.' Ewan shook hands, taking an immediate liking to the other couple. He smiled at Charlie, taking note of the braces on his feet. He'd seen them before and guessed the little boy had been born with club feet. 'And you too, Charlie.'

The child solemnly shook his hand then hurried away, heading straight for the apple tree. Hannah laughed as she dropped her bag onto the table. 'I wondered how long it would be before he made for the swing. He loves it!'

Everyone laughed as she raced after him. Ewan remained standing as the others sat down. 'It's time I was on my way. Good to see you all again, and to meet you and Hannah,' he added, smiling at Tom.

'Ditto,' Tom said, returning his smile. 'I don't know if Becky has mentioned it, but Charlie is being christened next Sunday. We're having everyone back to ours for lunch afterwards and it would be great if you could join us, Ewan.'

'Oh, but…'

'I don't think…' Ewan stopped when he and Becky both spoke at once. He shrugged when he saw the surprise on Tom's face. 'What we're trying to say is that Becky and I aren't an item, if that's what you thought.'

'Sorry.' Tom laughed. 'My mistake. Still, it makes no difference. I know Hannah would love you to come along if you're free.'

'Thanks. I'm not sure what hours I'm working next week but I appreciate it.'

It wasn't strictly true. Ewan had seen the coming week's roster and although he couldn't remember all his hours, he knew that he had Sunday off. However, it seemed politic not to accept the invitation when he sensed that Becky wouldn't approve. He adopted a deliberately neutral expression as he turned to her. Maybe they would be friends and maybe they wouldn't, but one thing was certain—they would never be lovers.

The thought was far too unsettling. Ewan blocked it from his mind as he smiled at her. 'Thanks again for the coffee, Becky. I'll see you around.'

'I expect so.'

She returned his smile but there was no real warmth in it. Ewan guessed that she was merely going through the motions because the others were watching. He sighed as he headed up the path and got into his car. He may as well accept that Becky wasn't interested in him and stop worrying about it.

The next week flew past. Although Becky had agreed to work only mornings while Brenda was still there, she found herself doing extra hours most days. A couple of practices in the area had closed in the past few years and their patients had transferred to Bride's Bay's list. It meant that everyone was under a lot of pressure but Becky was glad, even if it did mean her spending less time than she would have liked with Millie. At least while she was working, she wasn't thinking about Ewan, and that had to be a blessing.

She had found it increasingly difficult to put him out of her mind since Sunday morning. Although she knew it was stupid, she couldn't help wishing that she hadn't lied to him about Steve's reasons for living in the city. She felt guilty about what she'd done and confused as to why she'd felt it necessary. After all, what difference would it make to Ewan if he found out that her marriage had been less than perfect?

By the time Friday arrived, Becky was worn out from worrying about it. When Mrs Rose arrived to have her dressing changed, she had to make a determined effort to appear upbeat.

'Come in, Mrs Rose,' she said, ushering the old lady over to a chair. 'How are you today?'

'Fine, thank you, dear.' Edith Rose winced as she sank down onto the seat and Becky frowned.

'Is your leg troubling you?'

'No, no, it's fine. I just get the odd twinge in my hip from time to time.' Mrs Rose adjusted her position and smiled. 'There. That's better.'

'Good.' Becky went to fetch the tray she'd prepared, making a mental note to ask her father to take a look at Mrs Rose. Although the old lady had made light of it, she suspected that her hip was causing her some discomfort. She carried the tray over to the desk and then donned a pair of gloves. 'I'll just remove the old dressing and see how the cut is doing. It may be a little uncomfortable, I'm afraid.'

'You just do what you have to, my dear,' Mrs Rose told her, stoically.

Becky peeled away the dressing, pleased to see that there was no sign of infection. Although the cut was deep, it was already starting to heal. 'That looks fine. Using a non-adherent dressing means that the new tissue that's formed hasn't been disturbed.'

'That nice young doctor I saw at the hospital insisted the nurse should use one of those special dressings,' Mrs Rose told her. 'She was going to put a gauze pad on my leg but he told her to fetch something else.'

'He was quite right,' Becky agreed, feeling a small rush of pleasure run through her. Although she knew it was silly, it was good to hear Ewan receiving praise. 'The last thing we want is delicate new tissue being disturbed because the wrong type of dressing has been used.'

'That's what he said.' The old lady laughed. 'You two would get on very well, my dear. You obviously have a lot in common!'

Becky smiled although she didn't say anything. It was unsettling to realise that she and Ewan held such similar views. She gently cleaned the area around the cut and then placed a fresh dressing over it.

'There, that's all done. If it carries on healing as well as it's been doing then it won't be long before you don't need any more dressings.' She straightened Mrs Rose's skirt then helped her to her feet, frowning when she heard the old lady suck in her breath. 'Is your hip bothering you again?'

'Just another twinge,' Mrs Rose assured her. However, Becky could tell that she was making light of how painful it really was.

'Would you like me to ask one of the doctors to take a look at it, seeing as you're here?' she suggested.

Mrs Rose shook her head. 'Oh, no, dear. There's no need. It's just a twinge, as I said.' The old lady smiled brightly. 'It's all part and parcel of getting old, I'm afraid.'

Becky laughed dutifully although she couldn't help feeling concerned as she saw Mrs Rose out. She found herself wondering if Mrs Rose's reluctance to have her hip examined had something to do with what Ewan had told her. If the old lady was worried that her son would have her admitted to a nursing home if he could prove she couldn't manage on her own, then she would be wary of admitting that she had a problem.

Becky decided that she would mention her concerns to the rest of the team. They held a weekly team meeting each Monday when everyone had the chance to talk over any problems that had arisen. She made a note to bring it up the following Monday, thinking idly that it would have been even better if she could have discussed it with Ewan. He always had such a clear view of any problems and she was sure that he would have come up with a solution.

She sighed. That was the *fourth* time she'd thought about Ewan in under half an hour. He seemed to be taking over her life and it had to stop. Ewan was history; whatever might have been between them was over and done with. If she said it often enough, hopefully her brain would get the message.

Although Ewan was used to hard work, he had to admit that he had never worked as hard as he did at Pinscombe General. The fact that they were carrying several vacancies meant there was extra pressure on the staff. He arrived early and left late, usually so exhausted that he could barely summon the energy to make himself a drink let alone a meal when he got home.

As for his social life, it was non-existent. Although several of the nurses had made it clear that they would welcome his attentions, he was far too busy to think about dating, or that's what he told himself. It was easier than admitting that he wasn't interested in them now that he'd met Becky again.

Saturday rolled around and he was working the two-to-ten shift. The other registrar had called in sick on Friday so Ewan made a point of arriving early. He was glad that he had when he saw the queue in Reception.

'What's happened?' he asked, looping his stethoscope around his neck. 'Has war been declared in Devon or something?'

'It seems like it.' Cathy Morrison, the senior sister, rolled her eyes. 'It's been non-stop ever since I got here at six this morning.' She plonked a case file on the counter. 'Can you take a look at this one first? She's been here almost three hours now and you know what'll happen if the bean-counters flag up that we've kept a patient waiting for that length of time.'

'We'll be marched outside and shot at dawn?' Ewan suggested, drolly.

'Worse. We'll be sent on a time management course!'

'Fate worse than death,' Ewan concurred, grinning. He headed to the cubicles and didn't leave them again for the next six hours. Cuts, bruises, fractures, burns: he dealt with the lot. By the time he was able to snatch a break, he had lost track of the cases he'd seen. As he made his way to the canteen, he found himself thinking that it was a good job he hadn't accepted Tom's invitation to the christening. After an evening like this, all he wanted to do tomorrow was sleep!

His heart gave an unruly little hiccup as he found himself tagging on a codicil. All he wanted to do was sleep…with Becky.

* * *

Becky took Millie to the beach on Saturday afternoon. Although it was rather dull and cloudy, at least it was dry. She helped Millie make some sand pies and then they went looking for crabs. There were several other families there and Becky couldn't help feeling a little wistful as she watched them. Although she intended to do everything possible to make sure Millie enjoyed a happy childhood, the fact was that she was a single mother and it would never be the same as Millie having two parents to love and care for her.

The thought immediately made her think about Ewan for some reason and she sighed because it was stupid to place Ewan in this context. Ewan had never made any secret of the fact that he wasn't interested in settling down. At least he'd known what he'd wanted, unlike Steve. Although Steve had professed to want a family, he hadn't been a good father. He'd been too self-centred, put his own needs before anyone else's, including Millie's. Even if the accident hadn't happened, it was doubtful if he would have stayed around long enough to watch Millie growing up.

In a strange way, Becky felt better for having faced the truth at last. In the past year, she had skirted around it, mainly because she'd known how upset her parents would be if they found out that her marriage had been a disaster. Although she still didn't intend to tell them, at least she had come to terms with it and that had to be a good thing. If only she could get over her guilt about the accident, maybe she could move on.

She took Millie home, feeling more at ease than she had felt for a while. Her parents were going out to dinner that night so she made Millie's tea. Although it was the little girl's favourite, she didn't eat very much and she refused the yoghurt that Becky offered her for dessert. She seemed tired and rather listless so Becky decided to put her to bed as soon as she'd had her bath.

She settled Millie in her cot, leaving the door ajar so she could hear her if she woke, then went downstairs and made herself some supper. As soon as she'd finished, she ran upstairs to check on the little girl, her heart turning over when she saw Millie lying stiff and rigid in the cot. Millie's lips were rimmed with blue, her breathing was laboured and when Becky felt her forehead, it was burning hot. Millie had suffered a febrile convulsion the previous year and Becky realised in horror that she was having another one.

Becky ran downstairs and tried to phone her father but the call went straight to voice mail. She bit her lip, wondering who she could ask for help. She needed to get Millie to hospital and she couldn't drive as well as look after her. After a moment's thought, she phoned Tom and Hannah. Hannah answered.

'Hannah, it's Becky.' Becky didn't waste time on pleasantries. 'Millie's having a febrile convulsion. Mum and Dad are out and I need someone to run us to the hospital. It will be faster than calling an ambulance.'

'I'll be straight there,' Hannah said immediately. 'Try to keep her cool in the meantime. You know the drill.'

'Will do.'

Becky left the door on the latch then ran upstairs, grabbing a facecloth off the rack in the bathroom on the way. She soaked it in lukewarm water then went into the nursery and sponged Millie's hands and face. The little girl was wearing only a cotton sleep suit but Becky slid it off and sponged her body as well. By the time Hannah arrived, Millie felt a little cooler and the rigidity in her limbs was starting to ease.

'How long has she been like this?' Hannah asked, slipping a thermometer under the child's arm.

'Ten, possibly fifteen minutes.' Becky bit her lip. 'It's all my fault. She seemed very listless when I put her to bed. I should have stayed and checked if anything was wrong with her.'

'You weren't to know this would happen,' Hannah said soothingly. She checked Millie's temperature and frowned. 'It's still very high. We need to bring her temperature down and as we can't administer any drugs orally, it will have to be done via an IV drip. Can you wet a sheet and wrap her in it? That will help to keep her cool while we get her to hospital.'

Becky soaked a sheet in warm water and wrapped Millie in it. Hannah had the engine running when she carried the little girl outside. The drive to the hospital seemed endless even though Becky knew that Hannah was going as fast as she could. Millie kept drifting in and out of consciousness although, thankfully, she didn't suffer another convulsion.

Hannah drew up outside ED. 'You take her in while I park the car. I'll be with you as soon as I can.'

Becky slid out of the car and ran inside. She looked round, trying to get her bearings. Reception. Triage. Treatment rooms…

'Becky? What is it? What's happened?'

All of a sudden Ewan was there and Becky felt a rush of relief hit her. 'It's Millie. She's had a convulsion,' she began then couldn't go on as the shock of what had happened caught up with her.

Ewan put his hand under her elbow. 'Through here.' He steered her into a treatment room, gently taking Millie off her and laying her on the couch. Pressing the bell, he summoned one of the nurses. 'I need a fan in here, please, and a fine bore cannula.'

He rattled off a list of what he needed, his tone

so calm and controlled that Becky felt some of her fear start to ease. Drawing up a chair beside the bed, he sat her down next to Millie. 'She's going to be fine, Becky. I promise you.'

He squeezed her shoulder, his fingers biting gently into her flesh, and she shuddered. 'I was so scared, Ewan.'

'I know.' Bending, he looked into her eyes. 'I know you're scared but I won't let anything bad happen to her. Trust me.'

He straightened up as the nurse came back with a fan and the rest of the items he'd requested. Becky took a deep breath as she watched him. Cannulating veins as tiny as Millie's wasn't easy, as she knew from experience, but Ewan didn't hesitate; within seconds the line was in and Millie was receiving the drugs she needed to lower her temperature. Ewan knew what he was doing and she trusted him to do everything necessary to help Millie. He would be exactly the same with any other child but she knew this was different. Ewan would do everything possible to help Millie because he cared about her.

And he cared about Millie because Millie was *her* daughter.

Becky's heart filled with warmth. Knowing that Ewan cared made such a difference.

CHAPTER FIVE

EWAN CHECKED THE monitor, nodding when he saw that Millie's temperature had dropped. Although it certainly wasn't the first time he had treated a child who had suffered a febrile convulsion, there was no point pretending that he hadn't been worried.

He sighed. Although he knew it was ridiculous to feel personally involved, he couldn't help it. Millie was Becky's daughter and that made a world of difference. Turning, he smiled at her, his heart aching when he saw the worry on her face. Becky had been through enough without having to contend with this as well.

'Her temperature's falling. Give it another half-hour and it should be back to normal.'

'Thank heavens.' Becky looked up, her hazel eyes shadowed. 'It's all my fault. I knew Millie wasn't herself and I should have kept a closer watch over her.'

'Now you're being silly.' Ewan drew up a chair and sat down. Taking her hand, he gently squeezed it, trying to ignore the rush of sensations that flooded his body. There was a time and a place for feelings like those, and this was neither. 'You're not psychic, Becky. You weren't to know that her temperature would shoot up like that.'

'No…' It was obvious that she didn't believe him and his hand tightened. He hated to think that she was beating herself up when there was no need.

'No,' he repeated firmly. He leant forward and looked into her eyes. 'You know as well as I do that a child can be perfectly fine one minute and running a fever the next. It could have happened to any child and it's just unfortunate that Millie's brain couldn't handle the rapid rise in her temperature.'

'The first time it happened, they told me that she'd grow out of it,' she said, obviously seeking reassurance.

'That's right.' Ewan managed to curb the urge to put his arms around her. Millie was his patient and Becky was her mother; he had to behave with professional decorum. 'Once the temperature-lowering mechanism in her brain has matured, it will be able to deal with any sudden rise in her temperature.'

He released her hand and stood up, determined that he wasn't going to let her know how difficult it was to maintain his distance. Becky didn't need any more pressure on her tonight.

'But until it matures, it can happen again,' she said anxiously. 'I'd rather you told me the truth, Ewan, please.'

'Then, yes, it could.' He sighed inwardly, realising that no amount of reassurance would fully erase her fear. 'That's why we advise parents to be proactive. At the first sign of fever, you need to give Millie liquid paracetamol and repeat the dose every four to six hours as necessary. Sponging her with lukewarm water and removing her clothing—as you did tonight—will also help.'

'That's what I was told the last time,' she said

in a wobbly little voice. 'Which proves that what I said was true. If I'd been more vigilant, this might never have happened.'

'You can't watch her every minute of the day,' Ewan said sternly. He shook his head when she went to speak. 'I mean it, Becky. It won't do you or Millie any good if you start being overly protective.'

He looked round when the door opened, summoning a smile when he saw Hannah. Maybe he was wrong to take such a hard line but he hated to hear Becky berating herself when there was no need.

'Millie's temperature is dropping. It shouldn't be long before it's back to normal,' he told the other woman, wondering if *he* was in danger of committing the same error. After all, Becky was a grown woman and she didn't need him looking out for her.

'That's great news!' Hannah turned to Becky and smiled. 'You must be so relieved. I know I would be if it happened to Charlie.'

'I am.' Becky managed to smile but it was a poor effort.

Ewan shrugged when Hannah looked at him. The thought that he was becoming far too involved had touched a nerve. He and Becky weren't a couple and it would be a mistake to imagine that she needed his protection. 'Becky thinks it was her fault this happened. I've told her it wasn't, but she isn't convinced.'

'A mother's angst,' Hannah said lightly, giving Becky a hug. 'If I had a pound for every time I've blamed myself when something has happened to Charlie, I'd be a rich woman!'

Becky laughed shakily. 'So it's not just me who feels guilty all the time?'

'Nope. It comes with the territory, love.' Hannah straightened up and glanced at her watch. 'I just need to phone Tom and let him know what's happening. Will you be sending Millie home once her temperature's back to normal or do you intend to keep her in?'

'I'd prefer to keep her here for a while longer just to be on the safe side,' Ewan explained. He hurried on when he saw Becky blanch. 'Not that I'm expecting anything to go wrong. However,

I prefer to err on the side of caution when I'm dealing with a child.'

'Quite right,' Hannah said firmly. 'I'll let Tom know that I'll be a while yet.'

'You don't need to stay,' Becky protested. 'We'll be fine, honestly.'

'I can keep an eye on them,' Ewan assured her. He didn't look at Becky mainly because he didn't want to see that his offer wasn't welcome. He cleared his throat, calling himself every kind of fool for allowing the thought to upset him. 'I'm here till ten, probably longer if no agency staff turn up, so I'll be on hand if Becky needs anything.'

'Well, if you're sure?' Hannah looked from him to Becky.

'You go,' Becky said firmly. 'It's the christening tomorrow and you must have loads to do.'

'That's true, although I'm happy to stay if you want me to,' Hannah demurred.

'I'll be fine.' She turned to Ewan and he felt his heart jerk when he saw the expression in her eyes. Far from disliking the idea of him being around, she actually seemed to welcome it. It was hard to contain his delight as she continued, 'Ewan will take good care of us.'

'I'm sure he will,' Hannah agreed, and there was something in her voice that would have made Ewan blush if he'd been the blushing sort.

He quickly excused himself and went to see what other cases were lined up for him, trying not to read anything into what had happened, but it was impossible. Becky hadn't wanted to get rid of him, amazingly enough. On the contrary, she had seemed pleased that he would be sticking around. Did it mean that she was having second thoughts about him? But second thoughts about what, exactly? About him becoming more than just a friend? Was that what *he* wanted?

He grimaced. Maybe he was very attracted to Becky, but he'd been in this position before. And when push had come to shove she had chosen to stay with Steve. If he was honest, he knew it had been the right decision too. Although he had felt things for Becky he had never felt for any woman before or since, he hadn't been ready to settle down. Becky had understood that, which was why she had decided to stay with Steve and it had been the right decision for her too. She had married Steve and been perfectly happy... Hadn't she?

Ewan sighed. He had no right to speculate on the state of Becky's marriage. Maybe he was looking for flaws because it was so hard to accept that she had loved Steve and was still grieving for him. He should take it as a warning, in fact, and not get any more involved than he already was. There was no point setting his sights on Becky when she was still in love with her late husband.

Becky checked her watch, frowning when she discovered that it was almost midnight. Leaning over, she laid the back of her hand on Millie's forehead. Although she could see from the monitor that Millie's temperature was normal, motherly instinct had her testing it the old-fashioned way. A smile curved her lips when she felt the coolness of her daughter's skin. It seemed that tonight's little drama had been successfully concluded thanks to Ewan.

As though thinking about him had conjured

him up, he suddenly appeared. He smiled when he saw what she was doing. 'Don't you trust the monitor?'

'Yes, but I just like to check for myself that she's all right.' Becky returned his smile, wondering if he realised that her attitude towards him had changed. Ewan had always been extremely perceptive and it wouldn't surprise her if he had noticed that she had softened towards him. How did she feel about that? she wondered, then realised that she was far too tired to worry about it.

'Well, if you want my professional opinion then I'd say she's fine. Her temperature's been steady for over an hour now and I can't see it rising again.' He made a note on Millie's chart, stifling a yawn as he put it back in the holder. 'Excuse *me*! I'm afraid all the late nights are catching up with me.'

What sort of late nights? Becky wondered. Did he mean that he'd been working late or that he'd been out enjoying himself? That thought immediately led to the next one; who he'd been enjoying himself with. It was surprising how unsettling she found the idea. She cleared her throat, not wanting to go down the route of imagining Ewan and some woman out on the tiles or, worse still, spending cosy nights in together. What Ewan did in his private life wasn't any of her business.

'So you think it's safe to take her home?' she asked, focusing on Millie.

'Perfectly safe.' He smiled understandingly. 'You're bound to feel anxious, Becky. It's only natural, but she's fine. Believe me.'

'I do believe you.'

She gave him a quick smile, afraid that she might give too much away. Maybe she did feel differently about him, less wary and more open to having him around, but she mustn't be silly. They weren't going to get back together, neither did she want them to. There were too many reasons why it could never happen, starting with the most important one of all, the fact that Ewan would probably want children some day, and children were the one thing she couldn't give him.

'You've been absolutely brilliant tonight,' she

said sincerely, her heart aching at the thought of never being able to bear another child. If she was guilty of causing Steve's death then surely she'd been punished for it? 'I'm really grateful for everything you've done for Millie.'

'I was only doing my job,' he said lightly, but they both knew it had been far more than that.

Becky felt heat rush through her when she saw the warmth in his eyes. There wasn't a doubt in her mind that Ewan genuinely cared about her and even if it was only the sort of concern one felt for a friend, she found it incredibly comforting. It was on the tip of her tongue to say something when one of the nurses poked her head round the door.

'There's a phone call for you, Mrs Williams. It's your father.'

'Oh, right. Thank you.' Becky stood up then glanced uncertainly at Millie.

'I'll stay with her while you go and speak to him,' Ewan offered. He stifled another huge yawn then grinned at her. 'I am officially off duty at last so I won't be called away.'

'Oh, right, thank you,' Becky said gratefully.

She made her way to the desk and picked up the phone. 'Dad, it's me. I'm sorry. I know I should have called you but I'm in ED and I had to switch off my phone. However, the good news is that Millie's fine.'

Becky couldn't help feeling guilty when she heard the relief in her father's voice as he relayed the news to her mother. She quickly filled him in about what had happened. 'As I said, Millie is fine,' she repeated. 'In fact, I'll be bringing her home shortly. Ewan's happy for her to leave so that's good enough for me.'

'Ewan? So he's there with you, is he? Ah, good. Good.'

Becky felt her cheeks bloom with colour when she heard him repeat that to her mother. She didn't have to try too hard to imagine how her parents would interpret it and wished she had made it clearer that Ewan was there purely in a professional capacity. She glanced round when she heard footsteps and felt her heart leap when she saw Ewan coming towards her. He was carrying Millie, snugly wrapped in a blanket. The little girl's head was resting trustingly on his broad shoulder, her small hand gripping tight hold of his shirt collar. They looked so *right* together that Becky felt a rush of emotions hit her.

This was what she might have had if she hadn't chosen to stay with Steve. She had turned her back on the wild attraction and excitement that Ewan had brought to her life and opted for a relationship that had appeared to be rock-solid. It hadn't taken her long to realise how wrong she had been.

Although Steve had projected an air of calm and control, it had been all on the surface. Underneath, he'd been a mass of insecurities. He had blamed others for his failings, unable or unwilling to accept responsibility when things went wrong. Living with him had been a strain; it had felt as though she was permanently on a knife-edge, waiting for the next outburst. She had done her best to hold it all together for Millie's sake, but after she'd found out about his affair, something inside her had died. She had felt like a shell of her real self—empty, hollow.

Now, however, as she watched Ewan coming towards her with her daughter in his arms, she realised that she didn't feel empty anymore. She felt alive for the first time in ages, filled with expectation, and it scared her because she knew it wasn't right. That it wasn't fair. She had nothing to offer Ewan. Nothing at all that he truly needed.

'Becky? Are you still there?'

Becky roused herself when she heard her father calling her. No matter how she felt, she had to make sure that Ewan didn't get hurt. 'Yes, I'm here, Dad. Sorry. As I said, I'll be bringing Millie home soon.'

'I wish we could drive over there and collect you but your mother and I had a bottle of wine with dinner,' Simon apologised.

'Don't worry. I'll get a taxi,' she assured him. She ended the call then turned to take Millie from Ewan, somewhat surprised when the little girl clung to him.

'She's exhausted,' Ewan said easily, settling the child more comfortably against his shoulder. He smoothed back her soft fair curls with a gentle hand. 'You're ready for bed, aren't you, poppet?'

Millie nodded, her thumb slipping into her mouth the way it always did just before she drifted off to sleep, and Becky sighed. 'You're right. She's worn out after all the excitement. The sooner she's tucked up in her cot, the better. I don't suppose you know the number of a local taxi firm, do you?'

'You're hoping to find a taxi to take you home?' Ewan said in surprise, and she shrugged.

'I don't have a choice. Mum and Dad went out for dinner tonight and had a drink so they can't drive over here to collect us.'

'We must have some phone numbers somewhere,' Ewan said slowly, then grimaced. 'Although I don't rate your chances of finding a driver who's prepared to drive all the way out to Bride's Bay at this time of the night. It's Saturday, don't forget, and all the cabs will be busy ferrying folk home from the local clubs and pubs.'

'I never thought about that,' Becky admitted worriedly. 'I don't know what I'm going to do if I can't find a cab, though.'

'I can always run you home.'

'Oh, no. It wouldn't be fair to expect you to do that, Ewan. You've been working all night and you're worn out.'

'In that case, why don't you stay at my flat tonight?' He shrugged when she didn't answer. 'It's just five minutes away from here so it would be the ideal solution. You can have Millie tucked up in bed in no time at all.'

CHAPTER SIX

'AND THIS IS the bedroom. You're in luck because I changed the sheets this morning. They might not be ironed but they are clean!'

Ewan drummed up a laugh. Inviting Becky to stay the night had seemed like the right thing to do but he couldn't help wondering if it had been wise. He was already far more involved than he wanted to be and surely this would only make matters worse. He drove the thought from his mind as he opened the wardrobe and took out a couple of pillows. He'd be a poor sort of friend if he hadn't offered Becky somewhere to stay in her hour of need.

'You can use these to stop Millie rolling off the bed.' He laid the pillows along the edge of the bed to form a barrier. 'That should work all right, I think, don't you?'

'It's fine. Thank you.'

Becky sounded a little breathless, but that could have been his imagination, Ewan decided as he watched her look around the room. He followed her gaze, inwardly sighing because there wasn't much to see. He'd been travelling for so long that he hadn't had a chance to acquire many possessions. A selection of clothes, a few books, the odd photograph of him taking part in some mildly risky adventure like bungee jumping. It didn't seem a lot to show for the past eight years, especially not when he compared it to what Becky had achieved. She had been married and produced a child. That seemed like a far more valuable use of the time.

It wasn't like him to wonder if he should have set himself different goals. Ewan had always known what he'd wanted to do and to suddenly find himself questioning his decision was unsettling. Anyway, it was pointless trying to rewrite history. Becky had chosen Steve, not him, and that was the end of the matter. He cleared his throat, ignoring the little stab of pain that thought engendered.

'The bathroom's on your right and the kitchen

is straight ahead, through the living room. I doubt you'll get lost as the place is so small but give me a shout if you need anything and can't find it.'

'I will. Thank you,' she repeated in the same breathy little voice that was starting to do funny things to his libido.

Ewan forced it back into its box because this wasn't the time for it to make an all-singing, all-dancing appearance. 'That's it then…oh, you'll need something to wear.'

He opened the wardrobe again and snagged a T-shirt off the shelf. It was faded from many washings, its original deep blue colour mellowed to a smoky grey, like the sky just before dawn. He tossed it onto the bed, trying not to imagine how Becky would look wearing it, the soft, pale fabric clinging to her body. That way lay madness, or so the saying went!

'You're sure you don't mind, Ewan?'

He was almost out of the door when she spoke and he paused reluctantly, not wanting to put himself through any more tests that night. He'd managed pretty well so far, but he wasn't sure how long he could hold out. Maybe it was the fact that he was bone-tired or perhaps it was having her here in his home, but it was proving an effort to keep his hands to himself and away from her.

'Of course I don't mind.' A quick glance back, an even quicker smile, then another step towards safety, and he began to breathe a little easier.

'It's such an imposition, though. Especially after…well, after what happened between us all those years ago.'

Ewan took a deep breath. He could feel it filling his lungs right enough but it achieved very little else. It certainly didn't erase those pictures in his head, the ones of Becky modelling his ratty old T-shirt, neither did it screw down the lid on the box his libido was trying to climb out of. If he was honest, the extra oxygen simply enhanced all the bad things he was thinking and did nothing for the worthy, like the fact that he was playing the good Samaritan by inviting her into his home.

'That's all over with, Becky. We've both moved on since then, so let's forget about it, shall we?'

He feigned a yawn, wanting to bring the conversation to a speedy conclusion. The last thing he needed right now was them going back over old ground. 'Right, that's me done for the night. I'll see you in the morning. Sleep tight.'

He closed the door, leaning against it for a moment while he gathered his strength. It would be the work of seconds to go back and discuss what had happened but what was the point? The past was the past and there was nothing to be achieved by dwelling on what might have happened, definitely no point wishing that the child who was sleeping in his bed tonight was theirs. Millie was another man's daughter, not his. She never would be his, either.

The pain of that thought stung but he ignored it. Going into the living room, he shoved the coffee table aside and set about converting the sofa into a bed. He'd forgotten to get himself a pillow or a blanket but it was too risky to go back for them. There was no point pushing himself beyond all sensible limits.

'I thought you'd need these.'

Ewan jumped when Becky appeared with a

pillow and a blanket in her arms. She dropped them onto the sofa and grimaced. 'That doesn't look very comfortable.'

'It'll be fine,' he assured her, picking up the blanket. He draped it over the sofa then smiled with as much cheer as he could muster. 'I'll be as snug as a bug in a rug, as my gran used to say.'

'I hope so.' She went to go then stopped. 'I know you said to forget what happened but I can't. I never meant to lead you on, Ewan, and I'm sorry if I did.'

'You didn't lead me on,' he said flatly, sitting down on the edge of the sofa. There was a broken spring digging into his backside but he welcomed the discomfort because it gave him something to focus on apart from his own turbulent emotions. 'The attraction was mutual.'

'Yes, it was.' She bit her lip. 'It took me completely by surprise, if I'm honest.'

'These things happen, Becky.' He shrugged. 'And at the end of the day you made the right decision by choosing to stay with Steve.'

'I wish I could agree with you.'

Ewan's eyes flew to her face in shock. 'I beg your pardon?'

'Nothing. I shouldn't have said that.'

She turned to go but there was no way that he was letting her leave after saying that. He shot to his feet and caught hold of her arm.

'Maybe not, but you did say it and I want to know what you meant. Weren't you and Steve happy?'

'Our marriage was like everyone else's—we had good times and we had bad ones too.'

Ewan could tell that she was fudging the issue and even though he knew it was a mistake, he was determined to get at the truth. 'More bad times than good from the sound of it.'

'A lot of marriages go through rocky patches,' she said defensively.

'And that's what you went through, is it, rocky patches?'

'Yes. Steve…well, he set himself very high goals.'

'There's nothing wrong with that,' Ewan replied, not wanting it to appear as though he was criticising the other man.

'No.'

She bit her lip. Ewan could tell that she wanted to say something else and held his breath. It had to be her decision whether or not she confided in him, although whether he would want to hear what she had to say was another matter. For some reason he couldn't explain, it would be incredibly painful to discover that Becky had been unhappy in her marriage.

'Steve and I should never have got married,' she said at last. 'That's the long and the short of it.' She looked up and her eyes were very clear as they met his, clear and so devoid of emotion that Ewan felt as though his heart was cracking wide open. To know that Becky had been hurt so badly was almost more than he could bear. 'I wasn't right for him, you see, not supportive enough, not interesting enough, definitely not *sexy* enough.'

She gave a bitter little laugh that cut him to the quick. It was all he could do not to beg her to stop, only that would have been cowardly. She needed to get this off her chest and he had to listen, no matter how agonising he found it.

'So what happened?'

'What you'd expect, basically. Steve had an affair.' She shrugged. 'That was why he was so keen to move to the city. All those times he was supposedly called back into work, he was actually seeing her.'

'How did you find out?' Ewan asked, sickened by the thought of Becky being treated so shoddily.

'It was common knowledge in the hospital so it was simply a matter of time before I got to hear about it.'

'What did you do then?'

'We had a massive row and I threatened to leave, but Steve begged me not to for Millie's sake. He said he didn't want her growing up without both her parents present.'

'And you agreed with him, I take it?' Ewan said flatly, doing his best not to show how disgusted he felt about the other man's behaviour.

'Yes. I couldn't bear to think of Millie suffering, so I agreed to give our marriage another go on condition that Steve never saw the woman again.' She shrugged. 'He swore their affair was over but the night he was killed, I found an earring in the car and it wasn't mine.'

Ewan cursed under his breath. 'What did you do?'

'Asked him who it belonged to. Oh, he tried to explain it away but it was obvious he was lying and in the end he admitted that he was still seeing her. That's what we were arguing about when the accident happened. If we hadn't been, he might have seen the truck in time to avoid it. So, in a way, it's my fault that he's dead.'

Becky took a deep breath. She felt strangely removed, as though it hadn't been her speaking, but someone else. Ewan didn't say a word, although that didn't surprise her. What could he say? Even if he tried to tell her that she wasn't to blame, she wouldn't believe him. He hadn't been there, hadn't heard the terrible things she and Steve had said to one another.

'That has to be the craziest thing I've ever heard!'

The anger in his voice shocked her. Becky stared at him in surprise. 'Crazy?'

'Yes.' He turned her round to face him, his

eyes blazing into hers in a way that made heat flow through her numb veins. 'You weren't responsible for his death, Becky. It was an accident. One of those awful things that simply happen.'

'You weren't there,' she said, shaking her head. 'You've no idea what we said.'

'Maybe I can't repeat it verbatim but I can guess.' He gave her a shake, not hard or roughly, just enough to emphasise the point he was making. 'Your husband had just admitted he was still seeing another woman so you were hardly going to smile and agree that it was perfectly all right, were you?'

'No '

'No.' Another tiny shake, another blast from those searingly hot eyes, and the heat inside her turned into a flood. 'You're only human, Becky. You were bound to feel hurt and angry. It was only natural that you wanted to lash out.'

'I kept thinking about what it would mean for Millie,' she murmured.

'That she wouldn't have her daddy around

while she was growing up?' Ewan said softly, and she nodded.

'Yes. The only reason I'd agreed to try and make a go of our marriage was because I didn't want Millie to miss out on having a proper family.'

'A lot of kids grow up without one parent or the other,' he pointed out. 'They manage fine, too. Anyway, I'm sure you and Steve would have reached some sort of an understanding with regard to Millie. I can't imagine that you'd have stopped him seeing her.'

'I wouldn't if it had been what he'd wanted. However, he made it clear that night that he wasn't interested in seeing her.'

'What! Are you sure?'

Becky nodded. 'Quite sure. As Steve put it, he was sorry that we'd ever had a child and if I thought he was going to spend the next umpteen years putting his life on hold while she grew up, I could think again.' She laughed harshly. 'Using Millie as the reason for us to stay together had just been an excuse. It turned out that the woman he was involved with was the wife of one of the members of the hospital board. It wouldn't have done his career any good if she'd been cited in divorce proceedings.'

'I don't know what to say.' He tailed off, an expression of pain crossing his face as he let her go.

'There's nothing to say, Ewan. Maybe Steve only said it because he was angry—who knows? But it isn't easy to forget it.'

'I can understand that.'

He sat down on the sofa, looking so shaken that Becky found herself wishing that she hadn't told him. Maybe it had helped to get it off her chest but it wasn't fair to have upset him in the process. She laid her hand on his shoulder, feeling the heat from his body seeping into her palm in a way that was all too familiar. Ewan had always generated a lot of heat, she suddenly recalled. In fact they'd used to joke about it. She had accused him of being hot-blooded and he had claimed that it only happened when he was with her.

She removed her hand, unable to deal with the memory. It hurt to know that she had given up all they'd had for what she had believed would be a secure and stable life. 'It's time I let you go to bed. Thank you again for letting us stay. I appreciate it.'

'It isn't a problem.' He summoned a smile but she could tell it was an effort. Her story had affected him even more than she had expected but it was too late to take it back.

Becky wished him goodnight and went into the bedroom. Millie was fast asleep. She felt her forehead but it was cool to the touch with no hint of fever, not that she'd expected there would be. Ewan would never have allowed her to take Millie home if there'd been a chance of her suffering another convulsion.

She sighed as she slipped off her clothes and picked up the T-shirt he had lent her. The cotton felt cool against her bare skin and, she felt her nipples peak as it slithered over her body and shuddered. It had been a long time since she'd felt any sexual stirrings but all of a sudden she was aware of her body in a way that surprised her.

Climbing into bed, she made herself comfortable but sleep proved elusive. Although the sheets and pillowcases were freshly laundered, she could still smell Ewan on them, that spicy, masculine aroma that was his alone. When she finally drifted off to sleep, her dreams were filled with pictures of them together but not as they used to be. These pictures were of a time that hadn't happened, of a time that must never happen. Maybe there was some vestige left of the old attraction they had felt for one another but it wasn't enough; it never would be enough to make up for the fact that she had nothing to offer him. She could never ever give him a child.

Ewan let himself back into the flat, taking care not to make any noise. It was just gone seven but he'd been awake for hours. If truth be told, he hadn't slept, merely lain awake thinking about everything Becky had told him. He still found it hard to take it all in but Becky hadn't been lying. She had told him the truth, every painful word of it, and it hurt to know how she had suffered and not been able to do anything about it.

He made his way to the kitchen, stopping dead

when he found her sitting at the table. She was nursing a cup of tea and he got the impression that she'd been sitting there, nursing it, for some time, too. 'What are you doing up so early?' he asked, plonking the carrier bags he was holding onto the worktop.

'I couldn't sleep.'

She gave him a quick smile but Ewan was aware that she avoided looking directly at him. Was she sorry that she had told him about her marriage? he wondered as he began decanting the contents of the first bag. Worried in case he told someone else? His mouth thinned at the thought that she didn't trust him to keep her confidences.

'If you're worried that I'm going to tell anyone about what you said last night, there's no need.' He ripped open a packet of coffee and spooned some into the cafetière, trying not to let his disappointment show. Becky had no reason to trust any man after what had happened, not even him. 'I have no intention of repeating what you told me, Becky.'

'I know that.' She met his gaze for a second

before she looked away. 'It isn't your style to gossip, Ewan.'

'Oh. Right.' Ewan wasn't sure what to say. If it hadn't been that keeping her awake then what had it been? He finished unpacking the first bag and started on the second.

'Are you expecting an army for breakfast?'

There was a hint of laughter in her voice and he felt his heart lighten. Glancing at the array of goodies he'd piled on the counter, he chuckled. 'I wasn't sure what you and Millie might fancy so I thought I'd better cover all bases.'

'So I can see.' Becky got up and came over to the counter. 'Croissants, bacon, cereal, yoghurt, fruit, eggs… Hmm, the only thing missing is steak.'

'Steak,' he repeated rather hoarsely, suddenly finding it difficult to breathe. Becky was wearing his T-shirt and he had to admit that it had never looked better than it did at that moment, the full swell of her breasts adding an extra allure to the washed-thin fabric.

'To go with the eggs, of course.' She gave a tiny giggle that made the hair all over his body stand to attention. 'You always claimed that steak and eggs was the perfect breakfast. It gives you a double hit of protein plus umpteen other benefits, or so you maintained.'

'Probably end up giving you a coronary as well if you indulged too often,' he said wryly because he could *do* wry even if he couldn't do much else. He added a pot of jam—to go with the croissants—to the pile then started on bag number three. Nappies, wet wipes and a packet of bibs emerged and Becky gasped.

'You really have thought of everything!' She picked up a Cellophane pack containing two little cotton sleep suits with butterflies embroidered on them and shook her head. 'You shouldn't have gone to all this trouble, Ewan.'

'It was no trouble. Anyway, they're all things that Millie will need this morning.' He rolled the bag into a ball and stuffed it under the sink, his heart turning over when he straightened up and saw the tears in her eyes. 'What's the matter? Have I bought the wrong size or something?'

'No. They're perfect.' She gave a noisy sniff. 'I just didn't expect this…any of it.'

Tears began to pour down her face as she swept a hand towards the worktop and Ewan did the only thing he could think of. Drawing her into his arms, he held her while she cried, feeling the shudders that racked her body. He had a feeling that it had been a long time since she had given in to her emotions and was suddenly glad that he'd been around when she needed comforting. If Becky needed a shoulder to cry on, she could have his. Willingly.

'It's okay, sweetheart. You have a good cry,' he murmured, stroking her hair. A few silky tendrils snagged against the rough skin on his fingers and he gently freed them before letting his hand slide down her spine. Whether he'd intended to urge her closer, he wasn't sure, but she took a tiny step towards him, just enough to bring her body into intimate contact with his, and Ewan felt his own emotions suddenly run riot. He could feel the soft swell of her breasts pressing against the wall of his chest, feel to the very second when her nipples hardened, and his heart ran wild. A lot of water might have flowed under the bridge but there were still feelings between them—that was obvious!

He didn't pause to think as he bent and kissed her, didn't give himself time to wonder if he was making a mistake. He just wanted to kiss her, just needed to feel the softness of her mouth under his once more. The years seemed to fade away as they stood there, their mouths joined, their bodies entwined.

Becky was kissing him back and that was all that mattered, the fact that she wanted this as much as he did. What happened next was in the lap of the gods, although Ewan was under no illusions that it was the start of something. He wasn't even sure that he wanted it to be. All he wanted was to hold Becky in his arms and kiss her, comfort her and, if he was honest, comfort himself too because what she had told him last night had put a dent in his own heart.

His mouth opened over hers, inviting her to respond, and desire surged through him when she did so. He guessed that Becky had no more idea than he had where this was leading but it didn't matter to her either. At this precise moment in time, this kiss was enough for both of them!

CHAPTER SEVEN

BECKY COULD FEEL her heart pounding, a fierce, wild rhythm that made her cling to Ewan. His mouth was so hot, so urgent and yet so tender as it plundered hers. Even in the throes of passion, Ewan was aware of her needs, put her first. He always had done.

Tears stung her eyes once more and she heard him murmur in concern. However, when he went to pull back, she refused to let him go. Wrapping her arms around his neck, she drew his head down, taking the lead this time as she let her tongue slide between his lips. She didn't want the kiss to end just yet. She felt safe in Ewan's arms, safe and wonderfully alive. After the emotional wasteland she'd existed in these past few years, it was a marvellous feeling.

'Becky, please.' His hands gently gripped her

shoulders as he set her away from him. 'I think we should stop.'

His voice was firm, but she could hear the desire it held and smiled. 'If it's what you really want.'

He groaned as he pulled her back into his arms and kissed her hungrily. 'Of course it isn't what I want! But I don't want us to do something we'll regret either.'

A chill ran down her spine. Tilting her head, she stared into his face. 'You're sorry this happened?'

'I don't know how I feel, if you want the truth.' He stepped back, his hand trembling as he raked back his hair. 'I didn't plan on kissing you. It was the last thing I intended, in fact.'

'And now you're having second thoughts,' she said as calmly as she could. It hurt to know that he regretted what they'd done, hurt far more than it had any right to do. She drummed up a laugh, loath to let him see how vulnerable she felt. 'I understand, Ewan, really I do.'

'Then I wish you'd explain it to me.' He sighed. 'I want us to be friends, Becky. I want us to meet up for coffee, maybe go out for dinner occasionally, do all the things that friends do. We had our chance and I'm under no illusion that we can be more than friends these days. Yet when I kissed you just now, it wasn't friendship I was feeling, believe me.'

'Maybe it was because of how we once felt,' she suggested, wondering if it explained why she had felt so aroused. It was years since she had wanted anyone the way she had wanted Ewan just now, so was it familiarity that had rekindled her desire?

'It was a blast from the past—is that what you're saying?'

His tone was sceptical but Becky didn't want anything to ruin her theory. Maybe the kiss had been wonderful but she'd be crazy to imagine it could lead anywhere. Ewan had his own life to lead, a future that would probably entail a wife and a family at some point, and she wouldn't do anything that might hold him back.

'Yes.' She shrugged, refusing to dwell on the thought of what the future held in store for him. She had no right to feel jealous of the woman he would eventually choose to be his wife and the mother of his children. 'Let's face it, Ewan, we were very attracted to one another, weren't we?' She gave a light laugh. 'I had a real crush on you, if I'm honest!'

'And like most crushes, it didn't last.' He laughed sardonically. 'Hmm, I think we should leave it there. I don't think my ego can take a battering this early in the day!'

Becky laughed as well, although her heart was heavy as she excused herself and went to get dressed. It was doubtful if Ewan's ego took a pounding very often. From what she had seen in the past, he was far too successful with women to suffer many setbacks. He could have his pick, in fact, so it was little wonder that he didn't want to get involved with her. After all, why should Ewan be interested in a single mother like her?

It was a sobering thought. Becky found it difficult to shake it off as she woke Millie and changed her. She carried her into the kitchen and sat her down on a chair. Ewan glanced round, holding up the pot of coffee.

'Want some?'

'Please.' Becky opened a packet of cereal then found a bowl and poured some into it. She added milk from the jug then went to get up to fetch a spoon.

'Here you go.' Ewan handed her a teaspoon, grinning when Millie began to bounce up and down in excitement. 'Someone's eager for her breakfast.'

'She loves cereal and this just happens to be her favourite,' Becky explained, helping the little girl spoon some into her mouth. She shook her head when Millie tried to take the spoon off her. 'No, let me help you, darling, otherwise it will end up all over the place.'

'Don't worry about making a mess.' Ewan handed Millie a spoon, laughing when she plunged it into the bowl, showering milk all over the table. 'It's not as though she can spoil the décor.'

Becky smiled as he shot a wry look around the room. 'You mean to say, this particular shade of red isn't to your taste?'

'I can't imagine it being to many people's taste,' he retorted. 'It's like living in a nightmare—there's pulsating red walls everywhere you look.'

Becky chuckled. 'I take it that you're planning to redecorate.'

'As soon as I find the time.' He took the croissants out of the oven and brought them over to the table. 'We're short-staffed at the moment so I've been working extra shifts. Hopefully, things will ease off soon, though.'

So he hadn't been out on the town; he'd been working. Becky hurriedly squashed the feeling of relief that thought aroused. She concentrated on helping Millie, smiling when the little girl finished her cereal in record time. 'You must have been hungry, sweetheart. Would you like a banana?'

''Nana,' Millie repeated.

'I'll get it.' Ewan reached over and took a banana out of the fruit bowl. Becky looked away when the hem of his polo shirt lifted an inch or two, affording her a tantalising glimpse of taut, tanned midriff.

'Thanks,' she murmured, willing her racing pulse to slow down. It was just a glimpse of bare skin, she told herself sternly. Nothing to get worked up about. However, it was surprising how difficult she found it to follow the advice. Whichever way she looked at it, Ewan still possessed the power to disturb her.

They ate their breakfast, chatting easily about this and that. Becky leant back in her chair when she finished. 'That was delicious! I'm afraid I made a bit of a pig of myself. Sorry.'

'There's no need to apologise.' Ewan grinned at her. 'I'm just in awe of the fact that you managed to eat *three* croissants. It takes a dedicated eater to manage that little lot.'

'Make me feel better, why don't you?' Becky retorted, and he laughed.

'I'm just teasing. Anyway, you could do with putting on a few extra pounds.'

It was the sort of throwaway comment that anyone might make; however, the fact that it was Ewan making it put a whole different spin on it. Becky couldn't help wondering if he found her new, slimline figure less attractive than her previous curves before she realised what she was doing. Whether or not Ewan found her attractive wasn't important, was it?

'If I keep on eating like this, it won't be long before I'll need to think about dieting,' she said lightly. She peeled a wet wipe out of the packet and wiped Millie's hands. 'Right, I'm going to get this little lady washed and dressed in one of those lovely new sleep suits you bought her.'

'You do that.' Ewan stood up and started clearing the table. 'Give me a shout when you're ready to leave.'

Was that a hint that she had outstayed her welcome? Becky wondered as she lifted Millie down from the table. Not that she blamed him if it was. After all, he had done everything possible to make her feel welcome. Maybe that kiss hadn't been part of his plan, but she could hardly object when she had been as eager for it as him.

She sighed as she carried Millie into the bathroom. It wouldn't happen again. Ewan had made it perfectly clear that he only wanted them to be friends and she should be pleased he felt that way. There was less risk of getting hurt if they stuck to friendship.

It was the right decision, the sensible one, yet Becky couldn't help feeling downhearted. Deep down, she knew that if the situation had been different she would have wanted more than friendship from him.

Ewan took his time as he drove Becky back to Bride's Bay. The roads were a lot busier than they'd been the previous week. This part of the coast was a tourist magnet and soon all the roads would be thronged with cars and caravans and trailers.

'Looks like the early summer rush is starting,' he observed, slowing down when the driver in front stopped to check a signpost.

'Give it a few more weeks and the roads will be packed,' Becky agreed. She grimaced when the car ahead indicated right and then turned left. 'People's driving doesn't get any better, does it?'

'They're wearing their holiday heads,' Ewan said lightly. 'The rules of the road take second place to the need to reach their destination.'

'They'll be lucky if they make it in one piece

if that's the way they drive,' she said tartly, and he laughed.

'Good job we locals know to give the tourists a wide berth.'

'A very wide one in some cases,' she said sharply.

Ewan glanced at her. 'Are you nervous about being driven after the accident?'

'A bit.' She sighed. 'I kept getting flashbacks in the beginning, although they've stopped now, thankfully. It's just at odd times that I feel a bit… well, anxious, I suppose.'

'I expect I'd feel the same.' He picked up speed, although he was careful not to go too fast in view of what she had said. 'Mum told me that you were quite badly injured in the crash.'

'That's right.'

She glanced out of the window but not quickly enough to hide the sadness on her face. Ewan couldn't help wondering what was behind it but short of asking her there was no way of knowing, and he wasn't sure if he should go down that route. They had already crossed boundaries he hadn't planned on crossing with that kiss and it would be too risky to cross any more that day.

They reached Bride's Bay and drove straight to the surgery. Ewan parked the car then lifted Millie out of the back. She chuckled when he buzzed her cheek with a kiss.

'Who's been a good girl, then?' he said, tossing her into the air.

Millie squealed in delight. "Gain, 'gain!'

Ewan laughed as he tossed her up again. 'So you're a little daredevil, are you?' He settled her in his arms then looked round when Becky joined them. 'She obviously enjoys a bit of rough and tumble.'

'Oh, she does. She adores it when Dad plays with her. He picks her up and swings her round, and she screams with laughter.'

'Men play differently with a child,' he observed wryly. 'We tend to be a lot more physical.'

'Which is what Millie loves.' She sighed. 'She's missed out on such a lot in the past year. It's a real shame.'

'She doesn't seem to have taken any harm

from it,' he said firmly, not wanting her to feel guilty when there was no need. 'Anyway, now she has your father to play with her, she'll soon make up for lost time.'

'Yes, although I'm not sure how long we'll be living with my parents.'

She led the way up the path and Ewan followed her, his heart sinking. It had never occurred to him that she might not stay in Bride's Bay and he found the idea strangely unpalatable.

'So you're thinking of moving?' he said as she let them into the kitchen.

'As soon as I can save enough money for a deposit, yes.' She took Millie from him and set her down on the floor. 'I'll have to rent, of course—I certainly can't afford to buy with property prices being so high. But my plan is to get a place of my own as soon as I can.'

'Here, in Bride's Bay, or further afield?' he asked, determined not to let her know how much he hated the idea of her moving away.

'Oh, here, or somewhere close by at any rate.' She filled the kettle and set it to boil. 'I love working at the surgery and I don't want to have to give it up, plus it will be so much easier if Mum helps me with Millie. Millie will be starting nursery soon but she'll only be doing half-days to begin with so I'll need someone to look after her for the rest of the time. Mum has very kindly offered to do it.'

Thank heavens for that! Ewan thought in relief, although he took care not to show it. 'It sounds like a good plan to me.'

'It's the best I can think of in the circumstances,' Becky said flatly.

Ewan bit back a sigh. It was obvious that Becky had never expected her life to turn out this way but it wasn't her fault she had ended up as a single parent. He was on the point of telling her that when Ros Harper appeared. She smiled broadly when she saw them.

'Ah, so you're back, are you? Good.' She bent down and picked up her granddaughter. 'And how are you this morning, poppet? You certainly gave your poor old granny and grandpa a fright.'

'She's as right as rain,' Ewan assured her. 'I know it must have been worrying for you, but, as I explained to Becky, Millie will grow out of the convulsions in time.'

'I'm sure she will.' Ros kissed her granddaughter's cheek. 'I'm just glad you were around, Ewan. Simon and I felt a lot happier once we knew you were there, looking after them both.'

Ewan wasn't deaf to the nuances in Ros's voice; neither was Becky, he suspected. It was obvious that it would suit Ros if he and Becky got together but it wasn't going to happen. He smiled politely, feeling that he should set matters straight.

'It was lucky that I was on duty last night and able to help. After all, Becky and I have been friends for some time.'

'Of course you have.' Ros seemed undeterred as she turned and smiled at her daughter. 'Do you want me to get Millie ready while you get changed? Tom and Hannah are expecting us around noon.'

'Oh, I'd forgotten about the christening party!' Becky exclaimed. She glanced at Ewan. 'Are you coming? I know Tom invited you and seeing as you're already here…'

She tailed off, leaving him to make the final decision. Should he go? he wondered. Or would it only make the situation more complicated? If he turned up with Becky, it wouldn't be only Ros expecting great things of them.

He shook his head. 'I think I'd better shoot off home. I've got loads to do after working all those extra shifts last week.'

'Oh, surely you can spare an hour?' Ros put in before Becky could say anything. 'Tom and Hannah will be so disappointed if you miss the party. They both said how much they'd enjoyed meeting you.'

'I enjoyed meeting them too but I really do have an awful lot to do,' Ewan countered.

'An hour isn't going to make much difference, though, is it?' Ros glanced at her watch. 'It's gone eleven already, so why not pop along and have some lunch and then go home? I mean, you'll have to eat whatever you're doing, won't you?'

Ewan knew when he was beaten and gave in as gracefully as he could. 'All right. I'll drop in to say hello and then shoot off.' He hurried on when Ros went to interrupt. 'Becky and I had a massive breakfast, as it happens. I'm not sure if I can manage lunch as well.'

'Oh, well, never mind. I'm sure Tom and Hannah will be thrilled to see you.' Ros smiled contentedly as she picked up her granddaughter and left.

Ewan sighed. 'Ever had the feeling that you've been outmanoeuvred?'

'Frequently. Mum's a master at it.' Becky's tone was wry. 'She does it so nicely, too, that it's hard to take offence.'

Ewan laughed. 'Don't I know it!' He sobered abruptly. 'You do realise that she thinks we're going to get together?'

'Yes. Don't worry, Ewan—I'll set her straight. There's no point her getting her hopes up about something that's never going to happen.' She glanced at the kitchen clock and grimaced. 'I'd better get changed. Make yourself a cup of coffee, won't you?'

She left the kitchen and a moment later Ewan heard her running up the stairs. He found himself a mug and spooned some instant coffee into it. The sugar was in a jar by the kettle so he added a spoonful to the mug, sighing as he realised that he needed to make it clear to everyone that he and Becky weren't romantically involved. Maybe people were hoping it would happen but it wasn't what either of them wanted....

Was it?

His heart seemed to leap into his throat. Did he want to be more than a friend to Becky? He knew that his answer should be a resounding no and the fact that it wasn't worried him. He didn't *want* to fall in love with her, certainly didn't *intend* to run the risk of getting hurt. Maybe her marriage hadn't been all it should have been but she must have loved Steve, otherwise she wouldn't have married him. She probably still had feelings for him, so it would be crazy to get involved with her. However, despite all that, he couldn't in all conscience put his hand on his heart and swear it wouldn't happen.

CHAPTER EIGHT

'BECKY, HI! HOW lovely to see you. And this must be your little girl—Millie, isn't it?'

Becky smiled as Emily came over to them. Emily had been the practice nurse at the surgery before she'd got married and moved to Paris. 'Hello, Emily. Lovely to see you too. Yes, this is Millie. Say hello to Auntie Emily, darling.'

Emily laughed when Millie promptly hid her face in Becky's neck. 'She's going through the shy stage, is she? Theo was exactly the same at her age.'

'I'm hoping that she'll grow out of it when she goes to nursery,' Becky explained ruefully. She looked up when a tall, dark-haired man came to join them. He had a little boy with him and the resemblance between them was unmistakable. 'No need to ask who you two are,' she said, smiling at them.

Emily laughed. 'As you so rightly guessed, this is my husband, Ben, and our son, Theo. They're like two peas in the proverbial pod, aren't they?'

Emily shot an adoring look at her husband and Becky bit back a sigh. She couldn't help feeling wistful when everywhere she looked there seemed to be couples madly in love with each other. Her gaze slid over Tom and Hannah, who were holding hands, and moved on to her parents, who even after thirty years of marriage had that special glow about them. Would she ever feel like that? Did she want to?

Her gaze alighted on Ewan, who was chatting to Lizzie, the receptionist at the surgery, and her heart jerked. Suddenly, all she could think about was that kiss and how wonderful it had been....

'Becky?'

Becky jumped when Emily jogged her arm. Colour rushed to her face as she realised that she'd missed what the other woman had said. 'Sorry. I was miles away. What did you say?'

'I was just asking if you were enjoying working at the surgery,' Emily explained, then grinned as she glanced over at Ewan. 'I take it that's Ewan. Ros told me he was here with you.'

'I…erm…yes, that's right. Mum persuaded him to pop in and say hello,' Becky said quickly. She took a deep breath and hurried on. Maybe that kiss had been wonderful, but there wasn't going to be a repeat. 'Millie had a febrile convulsion last night. I took her to the hospital—Hannah drove us there—and Ewan happened to be on duty and treated her. He very kindly drove us home again this morning.'

'They kept her in overnight?' Ben queried, frowning.

Becky groaned. Obviously, Ben was wondering what she was doing, bringing Millie to the party if the little girl had been ill enough to be admitted to hospital. 'No. She was well enough to be sent home, thankfully. It was rather late by then, though, and I couldn't get a taxi, so we stayed at Ewan's.'

'Ah, I see,' Ben said, smiling. He brushed Millie's cheek with his finger. 'It is good to know that you are feeling better, *ma petite*.'

They exchanged a few more pleasantries before Emily and Ben went to say hello to Mitch Johnson, the landlord of The Ship Inn, and his wife. Becky took Millie over to the sandpit. Charlie, Tom and Hannah's son, was making sand pies and Millie eagerly joined in.

'Looks as though someone's having fun.'

Becky didn't glance round; she didn't need to. She would recognise Ewan's voice anywhere, she realised, her heart sinking because it was yet another example of how deeply he had infiltrated her thoughts of late.

'Millie loves making sand pies,' she said lightly, doing her best to behave as though everything was fine, which in a way it was. After all, they had both agreed they weren't looking for more than friendship. Maybe that kiss had been unexpected but it had been a one-off and it wouldn't happen again. 'If Millie had her way, we'd spend every day at the beach.'

'Can't say I blame her. I'm a bit of a sand-pie freak myself.'

He crouched down and helped the children fill their buckets. When Charlie begged him to help them make a sand castle, he set to work with gusto. In a very short time they had constructed several turrets and were busily forming the base of the wall that surrounded them.

'You missed your vocation,' Becky told him, laughing. 'You should have been an architect, not a doctor.'

He grinned. 'I'm not sure I'd have been much good at it. The test of a good building is its stability and I think my designs may be somewhat lacking in that respect.'

The words were prophetic because just then one of the turrets gave way. Millie let out a loud wail as one side sheared off. Ewan swung her up into his arms. 'It doesn't matter, sweetheart. We can do it again. Don't cry.'

He tossed her up in the air and successfully distracted her. She was all smiles as she demanded that he do it again. Becky noticed several people watching them and smiling, and realised that they were putting two and two together and coming up with the wrong answer. However, short of announcing that she and Ewan weren't an item and that they had no intention of becoming one, either, there was little she could do. It was a relief when Tom clapped his hands and called for silence.

'I'm not going to bore you all by making a speech,' he began.

'That's a relief,' someone shouted, and everyone laughed.

Tom grinned. 'Exactly. I just want to thank you all for coming. Hannah and I really appreciate you taking the time to help us celebrate this very special day.'

There was a round of applause. Tom waited until it died down. Becky frowned when she realised how nervous he looked. From what she had learned of Tom, he wasn't the sort of person who suffered from nerves. Something was obviously going on.

'If I could beg a few more minutes of your time, folks, there's something rather important I'd like to do.' He turned to Hannah and held out his hand. 'Would you come over here for a second, darling?'

'What's going on?' Hannah demanded as she took Tom's hand. 'You're up to something, Tom Bradbury. I can tell!'

'I am indeed.' He suddenly dropped to one knee. 'Hannah Morris, will you do me the great honour of becoming my wife?'

A collective gasp broke out from all the guests. Without even thinking about it, Becky reached for Ewan's hand as she waited to hear what Hannah would say. She heard a phone ring and glanced round in time to see her father take his mobile out of his pocket but she was more concerned about Hannah's answer than anything else.

'Of course I'll marry you.' Hannah sounded indignant. 'I can't believe you thought I wouldn't!'

A huge cheer erupted as Tom swept Hannah into his arms and kissed her. Becky cheered as well, thrilled to have been witness to such a happy event.

Ewan laughed. 'There's nothing like a spot of old-fashioned romance to cheer everyone up.'

'There certainly isn't.' Becky turned and hugged him then realised what she was doing. 'Oh, I'm sorry…'

'Don't apologise. It's a time for hugs, I'd say.'

He hugged her back, making it appear so natural that any doubts she had fled. After all, friends often hugged one another and that was what she and Ewan were, friends. It was only when she caught her mother's eye and saw the smile that Ros bestowed on them that she realised how other people might interpret it. It was a relief when her father appeared and she and Ewan broke apart.

'That was Ambulance Control on the phone,' Simon announced. 'There's been an incident at Bride's Bay Manor—a coach carrying a party of holidaymakers has collided with a car. There's several dozen people injured apparently and Ambulance Control has asked if we can attend until the ambulances get there.'

'Do we know what sort of injuries they've sustained?' Ewan asked immediately.

'No. Details are sketchy, I'm afraid. We'll have to wait until we arrive to see what's happened.' He looked round when Tom and Hannah came to join them. Emily and Ben had followed them and they all listened intently while Simon recounted what had happened.

'Typical,' Hannah snorted. 'Put a whole load

of medics together and it's guaranteed there'll
be some sort of emergency!'

'At least it saves us having to make umpteen
phone calls to rally the troops,' Ewan pointed
out, grinning.

Tom laughed. 'Good point. So how do you
want to play this, Simon?' He glanced at the
others. 'Hannah and I can give Ben and Emily
a lift—that's assuming you're both coming.'
He carried on when the other couple nodded.
'Which means there's room for Becky and Ewan
in your car even if you need to bring extra supplies.'

In a very short time everything was arranged.
Ros and Lizzie had offered to look after the children, and Marie and Mitch Johnson had insisted
on taking care of the buffet so that lunch could
go ahead. All the guests then lined up outside
and waved them off.

Becky shook her head as they drove back to
the surgery. 'It's such a shame that Tom and
Hannah's day has been ruined.'

'I doubt this will have spoiled it,' Ewan said.
He was sitting in the front and he turned to look

at her. 'From the looks on their faces, it will take more than a call-out to take the shine off today. I don't think I've ever seen a couple who looked so happy, have you?'

'No.' Becky summoned a smile but Ewan's words had merely highlighted her earlier thoughts. Tom and Hannah were happy together, as were Emily and Ben. They'd each found the person they loved and their lives were all the richer for it.

She bit her lip as Ewan turned to face the front again. She'd thought she had found that sort of happiness with Steve but she had been wrong. Now she was in no position to look for that kind of a relationship when she had so little to offer anyone. She was a single mother who couldn't have any more children; what man would be interested in her?

Her eyes rested on the back of Ewan's head as sadness swept over her. Ewan certainly wasn't.

'Lady on the coach complaining of severe pain in her right leg. I think it may be a fractured femur.'

'I'll take a look.'

Ewan followed Becky over to the coach. The accident had happened close to the entrance to Bride's Bay Manor, a beautiful Tudor manor house that had been gifted to the nation by its former owners. Most of the passengers had been brought into the grounds for safety and everywhere he looked there were people sitting or lying on the grass. Although it appeared rather chaotic, it was, in fact, all very organised.

Becky and Emily had been performing triage ever since they'd arrived, sorting out the most seriously injured so they could be seen first. Thankfully, there didn't appear to be anything life-threatening. Cuts, bruises, a couple of fractures—much as could be expected from this type of incident. Ewan was confident that once he had dealt with this patient, he'd be able to start on the walking wounded.

He climbed aboard the coach and knelt down beside the woman and smiled at her. 'Hello, there. My name's Ewan and I'm a doctor. Becky tells me that your leg is hurting. May I take a look?'

'Sandra Fielding.'

The woman offered him her hand which he shook. She was very pale and her skin felt cold and clammy. Ewan glanced at Becky. 'Can you put in a line, please, Becky? Sandra could do with some extra fluids.'

Becky nodded, immediately understanding. Ewan set about examining the woman, pleased that he hadn't needed to elaborate. Sandra was exhibiting all the classic signs of shock, which could mean that she was bleeding internally. The fluid would help to compensate for what she was losing but it did mean that time was of the essence. The sooner she was transferred to hospital, the better.

He gently examined Sandra's thigh, unsurprised when he discovered that it was very swollen. It was obviously extremely painful, too, because Sandra winced even though he applied minimum pressure. With a fractured femoral shaft, like this, there was often extensive blood loss from the bone so he was relieved when Becky quietly informed him that the line was set up.

'Thanks.' He smiled at her, thinking how pretty she looked. She was still wearing the dress she had worn for the party, a soft green cotton overprinted with a pattern of vivid pink roses. Her hair was caught up into a loose knot, a few honey-gold strands falling around her face as she knelt down to check their patient's pulse. She looked so lovely that Ewan felt his heart surge before he determinedly brought it under control. They were here to do a job, not so he could indulge in his own little fantasies.

'It looks like your femur is fractured, Sandra,' he explained, adopting his most professional tone so that his attention would be less likely to wander again. Opening his backpack, he took out a vial of morphine. 'That's why you're in so much pain. I'm going to give you something to make you more comfortable. Have you had morphine before? It can make you feel rather sick but I can give you another drug that should help with that.'

'I've never had it before,' Sandra said anxiously.

'In that case we won't take any chances.' He

added metoclopramide—an antiemetic—to the syringe. Becky swabbed Sandra's arm and he slid in the needle. 'You'll feel a lot more comfortable in a few moments,' he assured her, putting the used syringe into the sharps box.

'What will happen about my leg?' Sandra asked. 'Will they put a plaster on it when I get to the hospital?'

'Obviously, it will need to be X-rayed but once the doctors know what they're dealing with, they'll decide on the best course of treatment,' Ewan said gently. He knew from past experience that people often reacted badly when they were told they might need an operation so he decided not to go down that route. However, it appeared that Sandra wanted to know exactly what she might have to face.

'So what will the treatment entail?' she demanded.

'The usual way to repair a fracture like this is to realign the ends of the bone and pin them together. It's done under a general anaesthetic so it isn't as painful as it sounds. Sometimes surgery isn't necessary and the bone can be manipulated into place and supported with a splint. The leg is then put in traction to make sure the bone heals correctly.'

'But that will take weeks!' Sandra exclaimed. 'I could end up stuck in hospital for ages.'

Ewan frowned when he realised how upset she sounded. Although nobody liked the idea of being hospitalised, her reaction seemed way over the top. He glanced at Becky and raised his brows, wondering if she could shed any light on the problem.

'You'll only be kept in for as long as is necessary,' Becky said soothingly.

'I know. I'm just being silly.' Tears welled in Sandra's eyes and Ewan saw Becky reach over and pat her hand.

'Of course you're not being silly. No one wants to end up in hospital.'

She gave the older woman a warm smile and Ewan looked away when he felt his heart give that crazy little lurch it had started doing recently. He couldn't believe how aware he was of Becky, how responsive he was to her every look, her every smile. He'd dated his fair share of women over the years but not one of them had had this effect on him.

It was a disquieting thought, all the more so in view of the fact that they'd agreed they weren't looking for romance. Even if he had wanted to get together with Becky—which he didn't!—she wouldn't welcome his advances...

Although she hadn't exactly pushed him away when he'd kissed her, had she? a small voice whispered mischievously in his ear.

Ewan ground his teeth as he put the sharps box into the bag. He and Becky weren't going to rekindle their relationship. End of story. 'I'm sure you won't be kept in hospital for longer than is absolutely necessary,' he said firmly. 'If there's a problem about you being away from home then the social work team should be able to help. They can make arrangements if there's someone dependent on you for their care, or even a pet that needs looking after.'

'It's not that. I live on my own and I don't have any pets,' Sandra informed him.

Ewan smiled encouragingly. Despite what Sandra had said, he could tell there was something troubling her. 'So what's the problem? It would be better if you got it off your chest and then you'll be able to concentrate on getting better.'

'You two young people will probably think I'm being very silly but I have a date next week, you see, and now I won't be able to go.'

'A date?' Ewan repeated, nonplussed.

'Yes. I'm a widow and it's the first time I'll have been out with a man since my husband died. Edward—that's the gentleman I'm supposed to be meeting—is an old friend from way back. He and I used to work together. We got on really well, but Edward was engaged to his late wife at the time, so nothing ever came of it...'

She tailed off, leaving them to fill in the gaps, which Ewan did only too easily. He glanced at Becky and could tell from her expression that she was very aware of how the situation mirrored their own.

'And now the two of you have met again?' Ewan said gently.

'Yes. Edward contacted my daughter. He sent Louise an email. He'd been trying to find me for a while, apparently. Anyway, it was Louise who persuaded me to meet him. I wasn't sure, but she insisted, so we arranged to meet on Monday night for dinner.' Sandra sighed. 'Edward wanted it to be sooner but I'd booked this holiday and I didn't want to cancel it and lose the money. Now I won't be able to go.'

'Why not phone Edward and explain what's happened?' Becky suggested. 'I'm sure he'll understand and you can arrange to meet some other time.'

'That's the problem, though. Edward lives in Canada now and he's due to fly home on Tuesday. There won't be another time.'

Sandra fell silent, obviously upset at the thought of them not being able to renew their friendship. The first of the ambulances had started to arrive so Ewan went outside and flagged one down. He knew the crew and quickly explained what treatment the patient had received then helped them fit an inflatable splint to Sandra's leg in readiness for the journey. In a very short time Sandra was being driven away.

Becky sighed as she watched the ambulance disappear. 'I feel so sorry for her, don't you? She was obviously upset at the thought of not seeing this Edward again.'

'Yes. There but for the grace of God, eh?' Ewan replied, picking up his backpack.

'Sorry?' Becky looked quizzically at him.

'I simply meant that if I hadn't spotted you at the airport then we might never have met again.'

'No, I don't suppose we would,' she agreed quietly. 'It's funny how these things turn out, isn't it?'

'It is indeed.' He summoned a smile, aware that the conversation was in danger of becoming a shade too heavy. Although there was little doubt that his mother would have informed him that Becky was back in Bride's Bay, he couldn't help wondering if he would have followed up the information.

Would he have sought her out? he asked himself as they headed over to the next casualty. Or would he have played safe and stuck to the status quo? He had been caught off guard when he'd seen Becky in Christchurch and hadn't stopped to weigh up the consequences of his actions. He'd been determined to speak to her and he had, but had it been the right thing to do? Had it been wise?

He sighed. Only time would tell, but it was unsettling to realise that one impulsive decision could affect the rest of his life.

CHAPTER NINE

MOST OF THE guests had left by the time they returned to Tom and Hannah's house. There were just Becky's mother and Lizzie left, looking after the children, plus Mitch and Marie, from The Ship Inn, who had stayed behind to clear up the remains of the lunch. Becky plopped down onto a deck chair, feeling completely exhausted. She and Ewan had treated at least a dozen people and the pace was starting to tell on her.

'I don't know about you but I'm shattered.' Ewan flopped down onto the grass beside her and groaned. 'And here was I thinking I'd have a nice, relaxing day off. Remind me not to count my proverbial chickens next time, will you?'

Becky chuckled. 'Stop complaining. You know you enjoyed every moment.'

'Hmm, I'd argue the toss with you about that if I could summon up enough energy.'

He gave her a lazy grin and Becky felt her heart squeeze in an extra beat. Ewan had always had a particularly sexy smile, the sort of smile that was guaranteed to make any woman's knees go weak, and hers were no exception. She struggled to her feet, not wanting to go down that route when it would only lead to a dead end. There was no mileage in recalling all the things she found so attractive about him.

'I'd better go and rescue Mum and Lizzie. They must be frazzled after having to look after the little horrors all afternoon.'

'I bet they've enjoyed every second,' Ewan countered. 'If your mum is anything like mine, she probably adores being a hands-on granny.'

'She does but even so…' Becky shrugged, not wanting to explain that it was more for her own peace of mind that she needed to get away. She had enjoyed working with Ewan, enjoyed it far too much. His skill as a doctor had never been in doubt and today he had demonstrated so many other qualities as well.

She sighed as she went to find her mother. Ewan had been kindness itself as he had dealt with the casualties. He had listened to what they'd had to say and shown no hint of impatience as each had repeated how shocked they'd been when the accident had happened. She knew that it would have helped them enormously to tell him about their experiences and couldn't help wishing that she'd been able to do the same after her own accident. If only she'd had Ewan there offering reassurance, maybe she would have dealt with the aftermath far better than she had done.

The thought troubled her as she collected Millie. Maybe it would have helped to talk about the accident but it wouldn't have changed the outcome. No amount of reassurances could make up for the fact that she would never be able to have another child. She cuddled Millie close as she carried her outside, knowing how selfish it was to feel this way. So many women were unable to have a child of their own and she was one of the lucky ones, but she couldn't help it. She had always hoped to have more children, although, now that she thought about it, she doubted if Steve would have agreed. Steve had found it taxing enough to cope with just one child. How on earth had she ever thought he was ideal husband material?

Her gaze rested on Ewan, who was lying spreadeagled on the grass, as a wave of regret washed over her. Her life could have turned out very differently if she'd chosen Ewan.

Ewan closed his eyes, enjoying the warmth of the sun playing over his body. This latest incident coming on top of an already busy week had left him feeling drained. He was looking forward to going home and putting his feet up but first he needed to check how Becky and Millie were getting home.

A shadow fell over him and he opened his eyes, squinting against the sun's glare. Becky was standing beside him and his heart gave its customary little hiccup. Even though there was no chance of them getting back together, he couldn't help responding to her. It was as though he was genetically programmed to react; Becky was around so it was all systems go.

He rolled to his feet, suddenly impatient with

himself. He was acting like an idiot and it had to stop. 'I take it your mum and Lizzie survived?' he said drolly, reaching out to tickle Millie under her chin.

'Just.' Becky treated him to a smile and off it went again, his pesky heart and its hiccups. Ewan just managed to suppress the curse that tried to escape, calling himself every kind of a fool instead. He and Becky were friends—period.

'Looking after a bunch of under-fives takes some doing, although your mother must be well versed in the art seeing as you and your brother are twins. I have to take my hat off to her. Coping with two little ones must be a major feat.'

'I'm sure you're right.'

Becky gave him another smile but some of the shine seemed to have gone out of it and he frowned. He had a feeling that his comment had touched a nerve although he had no idea why. However, before he could attempt to find out, Tom and Hannah appeared.

'There you are. We were hoping you hadn't left yet.' Tom said, grinning at them.

'I was just thinking about making tracks, actually,' Ewan admitted, relieved that he hadn't had the chance to say anything. He needed to remain detached if he was to stick to their plan of being friends. Something warned him that it wouldn't work if he got too involved in Becky's affairs.

'Oh, can't you hang on a bit longer?' Hannah implored him. She glanced at Tom and Ewan felt his heart ache when he saw the love in her eyes.

'It sounds as though you two are up to something,' he said jovially, avoiding looking at Becky. It wouldn't help to recall the way Becky had used to look at him all those years ago.

'We just thought that it would be nice to celebrate our engagement properly.' Hannah laughed. 'Tom had it all planned, apparently— champagne, toasts, the ring—but everything got hijacked when we were called out.'

'So what were you thinking of doing?' Becky asked and Ewan knew—he just knew!—that she'd been thinking the same thing.

His heart began to pound so that he missed what Hannah said. It was only when he realised that she and Tom were looking expectantly at him that he rallied. So what if Becky *had* been remembering how they'd felt about one another? It wouldn't change what had happened, certainly wouldn't alter the fact that she had chosen another man and not him.

'Sorry, I missed that. It must be my age. I can't stand the pace any more and tend to drift off at the least opportunity.'

'Less your age than the fact that you're worn out after having your day off ruined,' Tom said ruefully. 'I don't blame you if you think twice about accepting another of our invitations, although I do hope you'll come tonight. It will be all very casual—just dinner and drinks at The Ship—nothing fancy. And I promise on my honour that no matter what disaster befalls the town tonight, you are excused!'

Ewan laughed. 'Can I have that in triplicate, please?'

'If it means you'll come then yes.' Hannah grinned. 'Everyone's coming: Ros and Simon, Emily and Ben, Lizzie and her husband. It would be such a shame if you and Becky weren't there.'

'I'm afraid it's out of the question,' Becky put in quickly. She shrugged when they all looked at her, Ewan included. Although he had his suspicions about why she didn't want to go, he needed them confirmed. It might help him deal with this situation a bit better if he kept on reminding himself that Becky wasn't keen to spend any time with him.

'If Mum and Dad are going, there'll be no one to look after Millie,' she explained.

'Can't you take her along?' Ewan heard himself say, and blinked in surprise. Where had that come from? Surely he should be backing her up rather than making suggestions if he intended to keep his distance. He opened his mouth to backpedal but Hannah beat him to it.

'Of course you must bring her. We're taking Charlie and I know for a fact that Emily and Ben are intending to bring Theo along. Millie won't be on her own. She'll have a couple of cohorts there to help her create chaos!'

Tom and Hannah went off to speak to Mitch and Marie, who were about to leave. They seemed to have taken it for granted that everything was sorted out and short of making a fuss, Ewan realised, there was nothing they could do about it. He glanced at Becky and grimaced. 'Sorry. I wasn't much help, was I? It sort of… well, crept out.'

'It doesn't matter,' Becky said shortly. She settled a sleepy-looking Millie onto her hip and glanced round. 'I'd better go and find my parents. Millie will need a nap if I'm taking her out tonight.'

'I can run you home if they're not ready to leave yet,' Ewan offered, but she shook her head.

'No. It's fine. Thank you.'

She gave him a tight little smile and his heart ached when he saw how strained it was. It was obvious that Becky didn't relish the idea of them spending any more time together and he couldn't blame her. She'd made her feelings clear and he didn't need it spelt out. She wasn't interested in him in any way apart from as a friend and even that wasn't guaranteed.

It should have been a relief to know that but as he said his goodbyes, Ewan's heart was heavy.

Becky had been an important part of his life and it was hard to accept that he had been such a minor part of hers.

Becky settled Millie in her cot for a nap then went to lie down, hoping that a rest would help her relax. She would have preferred not to go to the engagement party but she simply couldn't think of an excuse not to attend. Even if Ewan hadn't suggested she should take Millie along, Hannah would have done, so there was no point blaming him. In fact, Ewan wasn't to blame for any of the things that had been plaguing her recently.

She sighed. Choosing to stay with Steve rather than allow her relationship with Ewan to develop had been her decision. She had opted for security, sure in her own mind that it had been the right decision, but look how it had turned out. Her marriage had been a disaster and she couldn't help wondering how different her life would have been if she had followed her heart rather than her head. She had been on the point of falling in love with Ewan, had known that he had felt the same about her, and she'd panicked.

Ewan hadn't been good husband material. He'd wanted to travel, see the world and explore what it had to offer. It had been so different from what she had always wanted—marriage, a home and a family—and she had been scared. It had seemed safer to stick to her plans even though it had hurt unbearably to let Ewan go. She could only imagine how hurt and angry he must have felt too, yet he hadn't tried to take it out on her when she had told him her decision. He had treated her with kindness and understanding—all those wonderful qualities that made him the man he was. Ewan stood head and shoulders above other men. He always had done.

It was painful to face up to the fact that she had made a terrible mistake. Becky was relieved when her mother tapped on the door.

'Are you asleep, darling?' Ros called quietly.

'No. Come in, Mum.' Becky sat up, smiling when she saw that Ros was carrying a tray of tea. 'Tea! How lovely. I'm gasping.'

'I thought you would be.' Ros put the tray

on the window seat and poured two mugs of tea. 'There's some homemade biscuits as well. I thought you might be hungry seeing as you missed lunch.'

'I am.' Becky took a couple of ginger biscuits off the plate. 'I don't know how you find the time to bake along with everything else you do.'

'Years of practice,' Ros assured her as she sat down on the bed. 'Millie's flat out. I just popped in to check on her and she's fast asleep.'

'Probably worn out after all the excitement of last night and today.' Becky dunked her biscuit in her tea, grinning when her mother tutted. 'Sorry, but they taste even better when you dunk them.'

'So your father keeps telling me,' Ros said dryly. She sipped her tea then looked at Becky. 'You and Ewan seem to be getting on extremely well. Several people remarked on how happy you looked together.'

Becky bit back a groan. So this was to be an interrogation, was it? Although she knew her mother meant well, it would be wrong to let her think there was something going on between her and Ewan. 'We're just friends, Mum, and that's all we'll ever be, too. So if you're holding out any hopes of a romance, forget it. Ewan isn't interested in me that way and I don't blame him.'

'What do you mean?'

Becky sighed, realising that she had boxed herself into a corner. Although her mother knew that she and Ewan had come close to dating in the past, Becky had never told her the full story. 'To put it in a nutshell, he asked me out but I chose to stay with Steve.'

'Really!' Ros exclaimed. 'I knew you'd been close when you were working at the same hospital but I hadn't realised you'd had a relationship.'

'We didn't…well, not really.' Becky flushed. 'I called a halt before things got too heavy.'

'I see.' Ros shrugged. 'It was a long time ago though, darling, wasn't it? And Ewan doesn't strike me as the sort to hold a grudge.'

'No, he isn't. But he's bound to be wary.' Becky felt a lump come to her throat, which was silly really. However, admitting how stupidly she had behaved seemed to make it all so much worse.

Ros patted her hand. 'I'm sure you only did what you thought was best.'

'I did. Ewan was a real flirt. He made no secret of the fact that he wasn't interested in settling down. He was keen to travel as well and I knew it wasn't what I wanted to do. It seemed better to not start anything with him then end up making us both miserable.'

'Then I'd say it was the right decision for both of you,' Ros said firmly. 'And I'm sure that Ewan thinks that too.'

'Maybe. But that doesn't mean we're going to get together now.'

'It's early days yet, darling, and I understand that you're still grieving, but the time will come when you feel ready to move on. All I'm saying is don't let Ewan slip through your fingers a second time, will you?'

Becky shook her head. 'It isn't going to happen, Mum. Even if Ewan wanted me back— which he doesn't—it wouldn't be fair.'

'Fair?' Ros put her cup down and looked at Becky in surprise. 'What do you mean by that?'

'Oh, nothing. Forget it.' Becky could have bitten off her tongue for making such a slip. She knew her mother wouldn't rest until she found out what was behind the comment.

'How can I forget it? What did you mean, Becky? Why wouldn't it be fair if you and Ewan got together?' Ros demanded.

Becky hesitated but all of a sudden the desire to tell her mother the truth was too strong to resist. 'Because Ewan will probably want a family of his own some day.'

'So why is that a problem? Are you saying that you don't want any more children?' Ros sounded perplexed, as well she might. Becky knew that she had to explain it all properly.

'No. I'd love to have more children but it isn't possible. You know that I sustained some really serious internal injuries in the crash?' She carried on when Ros nodded. 'Well, unfortunately, I had to have a hysterectomy. The fact is that I can't have any more children, Mum. I could never give Ewan a child, so it wouldn't be fair if we got together, would it?'

'Oh, darling, I am *so* sorry!' Ros got up and hugged her. 'Why didn't you tell your father and me what had happened? It must have been awful for you, having to go through something like that on your own.'

'I couldn't tell you, Mum. I don't know why but it was just too much to deal with on top of everything else.' Becky gulped. 'I suppose in a way I thought if I didn't talk about it, it might not be true, but it is. I'll never have another child, but I have Millie, so I'm very fortunate, aren't I?'

'You are indeed.' Ros kissed her on the forehead. 'Millie is a real sweetheart. Your father and I adore her, as you know. Anyone would, which is why I'm begging you not to rule out the idea of falling in love again.'

'I can't imagine it happening,' Becky said, wondering why the claim didn't ring true. She hurried on, not wanting to dwell on it right then. 'Although I haven't completely ruled it out.'

'Good.' Ros smiled at her. 'Ewan is wonderful with Millie, isn't he? And she seems to have really taken to him, too.'

Becky sighed. 'Stop it, Mum. I've already explained that Ewan and I aren't going to get back together so let's leave it at that, shall we?'

'If that's what you want, darling.' Ros stood up and gathered up the tea things. 'I'd better go and see if your father's awake. He's in the study, supposedly writing a report about the accident, but actually having a snooze. He'll need to get showered and changed before we set off for this evening's celebrations. We may as well walk down to The Ship if that's all right with you.'

'Fine,' Becky agreed.

She got up as soon as her mother left and went into the en suite bathroom, turning the shower to full blast so that the water bounced down onto the tiles. She stepped under the jets, hoping that the hot water would wash away all the thoughts that kept invading her mind, thoughts of her and Ewan and what they could and couldn't be to one another. She knew how it had to be, knew that they could never be together and why, but it didn't stop her wishing that things could have been different.

Ewan cast a quick glance into the mirror then picked up his car keys, wishing with all his heart that he had refused Tom and Hannah's invitation. He had never felt less like celebrating in his life, if he was honest. Maybe it was a knock-on effect from being so tired but his spirits were at an all-time low. He didn't want to spend the evening with Becky, knowing that she would have preferred to be with anyone but him. It would only rub salt into an already raw wound.

The fact that he still felt anything about what had happened all those years ago was unsettling. Ewan did his best to put it out of his mind as he drove to Bride's Bay. They were eating early because of the children and it was still light when he turned into pub's car park. Ewan felt his breath catch when he saw Becky heading into the pub. She was wearing a slim-fitting dress in a very deep blue—possibly sapphire or maybe azure—he wasn't that well versed in colours and couldn't be sure. However, what he could say was that it did all the things it should have done, highlighting the golden gleam of her hair and the trimness of her figure.

She was wearing high-heeled sandals with it and he groaned as he caught a glimpse of her shapely calves before she disappeared inside.

Tonight promised to be even more of an ordeal than he'd feared. He knew that Becky really didn't want him there. That was hard enough to contend with. However, the fact that he was doomed to spend the evening lusting after her would make it so much worse!

CHAPTER TEN

'YOURS IS THE chicken, isn't it, Becky?'

'Yes, that's right. Thank you.'

Becky took the plate that Marie offered her, relieved that they hadn't had to wait very long for their meal. With a bit of luck she should be able to make her escape as soon as dinner was over. They had already toasted Tom and Hannah, so nobody would think it rude if she left. After all, she did have the perfect excuse of needing to put Millie to bed, so give it another hour and she should be on her way home, thankfully.

'Salt?'

Ewan touched her arm and she jumped. Summoning a smile, she turned to him. It had been taken for granted that she and Ewan would want to sit together and the strain was starting to tell. Every time she moved, her arm brushed his arm or her thigh came into contact with his. Quite frankly, her nerves were in shreds and it was all she could do not to let him know how on edge she was feeling.

'No, I'm fine, thanks.'

Ewan put the salt cellar down. 'The food's always been good here, hasn't it? Thank heavens that Mitch and Marie haven't gone down the "fine dining" route.'

He drew imaginary speech marks round the words and Becky flinched as his shoulder brushed against hers. She murmured something, but she could feel her skin tingling from the contact. What on earth was the matter with her? Was she really so starved of sex that all it took was the lightest touch to arouse her?

The thought sent a rush of colour to her cheeks and out of the corner of her eyes she saw Ewan frown. She knew he was going to say something and hurriedly forestalled him. Turning, she smiled at Millie. 'Let Mummy help you with those peas, sweetheart.'

Picking up a spoon, she went to help Millie scoop up her peas but the little girl was having none of it. She pushed Becky's hand away, her lower lip jutting ominously. 'Me, me.'

'She's a determined little madam, isn't she?' Ewan laughed as Millie picked up a handful of peas and shovelled them into her mouth. 'Oh, well done, poppet. Clever girl for working out the best way to eat them.'

Millie beamed at him and Hannah, who was sitting opposite them, laughed. 'Looks like you've made a conquest there, Ewan.'

'What can I say?' He adopted a suitably modest expression. 'You've either got it or you haven't. Obviously, I'm a big hit with females under the age of two!'

Everyone laughed. Even Becky managed to dredge up a smile, knowing it was expected. It was clear that everyone believed she and Ewan were a couple and short of announcing that they weren't, she had no choice other than to go along with it.

'You should practise your technique and see if you can have the same effect on their mothers,' she suggested, setting off another round of laughter.

'Good idea.' Ewan grinned at her but his eyes were cool. 'I might just try that.'

The others all thought they were joking, of course, but Becky knew differently. She applied herself to her dinner but although the food was excellent, it tasted like sawdust. Ewan hadn't welcomed her advice and why should he have done? He didn't need her to tell him how to woo a woman. He could manage it perfectly well by himself!

The thought of all the women that he had wooed and won was even harder to swallow than her dinner. It was a relief when everyone finished and she could make her excuses and leave.

'I hate to be a party pooper but I really should take Millie home now,' she said, standing up. 'She had a really late night last night and I don't want her getting overtired.'

'Do you want me to walk back home with you, darling?' her mother offered.

'No, you stay and finish your wine.' Becky smiled around the table, deliberately avoiding Ewan's eyes. Although she knew she had no rights where he was concerned, it still hurt to

think about Ewan and all those other women.
'I'll see you very soon, I expect.'

'Too right you will,' Tom put in with a grin.
'Tomorrow morning at the surgery, bright and
early.'

Becky drummed up a laugh as she lifted Millie out of the high chair. 'It hardly seems worth
going to bed, does it?'

'Oh, I don't know.' Tom glanced at Hannah,
making it clear why he disagreed with that sentiment.

Becky smiled, although her heart was aching
in the most peculiar fashion. So what if Tom and
Hannah intended to celebrate their engagement
in time-honoured fashion? It shouldn't bother
her. 'I don't think I'll ask what you meant by
that!' she replied, adopting a deliberately upbeat tone.

She picked up her bag then glanced round in
surprise when she realised that Ewan had stood
up as well. He smiled at her but his eyes were
still rather chilly.

'I'll walk you home.'

'There's no need,' she began, but he didn't let her finish.

'I have to leave, anyway, and I'd prefer to know that you and Millie had got home safely.'

Becky's mouth thinned when she saw the approval on everyone's faces. It was obvious that they thought it only right that Ewan should see her home and, short of making a scene, there was nothing she could do. She popped Millie into her pushchair then led the way across the restaurant, nodding her thanks when Ewan opened the door for her because she didn't trust herself to speak. Didn't he realise that he was only making the situation worse by fostering the idea that they were a couple? She waited until they were safely out of earshot before she rounded on him.

'What are you playing at, Ewan? The last thing we need is people thinking we're an item!'

'They're going to think it no matter what we do.' He shrugged, his broad shoulders moving lightly under the thin cotton shirt he was wearing.

Becky felt her mouth go dry as she saw his

muscles ripple, and looked away. She didn't need this, didn't need any more reminders of how attractive he was. Ewan had always been fit but his body had matured in the past few years. Now there didn't appear to be an ounce of spare flesh on him. All of a sudden she found herself imagining how he would feel if she ran her hands over him: smooth warm skin, hard, toned muscles, a dusting of crisp dark hair...

She drove the images from her mind. She wasn't going to think about things like that! Taking a firmer grip on the pushchair, she headed across the car park, aware that Ewan was keeping pace with her. Even though she *really* didn't want him walking her home, she knew there was no point objecting. Once Ewan made up his mind, it was impossible to change it.

They walked back to the house in silence. Millie fell asleep almost immediately, worn out by her adventures. Becky unlocked the door then bent down and undid the harness. With a bit of luck she might be able to get Millie into bed without waking her, she thought as she carefully lifted her out of the pushchair.

'I'll fetch the pushchair in.'

Becky barely glanced at Ewan as he lifted it over the step. He could do whatever he liked—she didn't care anymore. She carried Millie upstairs and laid her on the changing mat, quickly stripping off her dress before popping on a clean nappy and a pair of pale green cotton pyjamas with bunnies on them. The little girl didn't stir as she settled her in the cot and covered her with a blanket.

'Night-night, darling,' she murmured, stroking the child's soft little cheek. It was at moments like this that she realised how lucky she was. Millie meant everything to her; she was her reason for living, the one thing that had kept her going after the accident when life had seemed so grim. So long as Millie was safe and happy, nothing else mattered, not what people thought about her and Ewan, or how she felt about him…

Her heart gave a painful little jolt. How *did* she feel about Ewan? There was no doubt that she liked and admired him. That she found him physically attractive as well wasn't in question either if tonight was anything to go by. So what did it all add up to? Was it possible that she was falling in love with him again?

Becky left the bedroom and went and sat on the top step, her legs suddenly too weak to support her. She didn't want to fall in love with Ewan. It would be a mistake for all sorts of reasons. However, she couldn't put her hand on her heart and swear it wouldn't happen, could she?

Ewan glanced at his watch and frowned. Becky seemed to be taking an inordinately long time putting Millie to bed. Maybe he should check if everything was all right....

And maybe he shouldn't.

He sighed when it struck him that Becky was probably doing it deliberately, spinning things out in the hope that he would get fed up and leave. Well, if that was the case then he didn't intend to disappoint her!

Opening the back door, he went to step out, then hesitated. Maybe it was silly, but he hated to think that they were parting on bad terms, especially when he knew it was mainly his fault. After all, Becky was bound to be sensitive about people misinterpreting their friendship. It was barely a year since she'd been widowed and it was only natural that she wouldn't want everyone to think that she had forgotten her husband.

Ewan went back inside. He made his way along the hall, pausing when he reached the stairs. Should he go and find Becky and apologise? Or would it be better if he left her a note? He didn't want to add to her distress so it was hard to decide. It was only when he happened to glance up and saw her sitting on the stairs that he made up his mind.

'Are you all right?' he asked as he went to join her. He sat down on the step below so that they were on eye level, his heart contracting when he saw the anguish on her face. It was obvious that she was torturing herself, unnecessarily, too.

'I'm really sorry, Becky,' he said, taking hold of her hand. Her fingers felt so small and cold and his hand tightened, wanting to instil some warmth into her flesh. 'I never meant to upset you.'

'Upset me?'

'Yes.' He sighed. 'I understand now why you

don't want folk thinking we're an item. I mean, it's barely a year since you lost your husband, isn't it?'

'Yes.' She bit her lip and Ewan felt even more wretched. To know that he had caused her all this heartache was very hard.

'I promise you that I'll make sure everyone knows the truth. In fact, I'll phone Tom tomorrow and set him straight, and ask him to tell everyone else.'

'If that's what you want, then fine,' she said flatly.

Ewan frowned. 'It's what you want, isn't it? I mean, that's why you're upset, because you hate the idea of people thinking that you're over Steve?'

She shrugged. 'I don't care what they think.'

'Really?' He bent closer. 'So if it isn't that which has upset you, what is it?'

'Nothing. I'm just tired, that's all.'

Ewan knew it was a lie and he wasn't prepared to let her get away with it. 'I don't believe you, Becky. Something's wrong and I want to know what it is.' He dredged up a smile. 'That's what friends are for, to share problems and give you a boost when you need it.'

'Do you think we can stick to being friends, Ewan?' She looked at him and Ewan felt his pulse leap when he saw the awareness in her eyes. It took every scrap of willpower not to respond but he'd caused enough damage for one evening.

'If it's what we both want, then, yes, I do.' He hesitated but he had to ask even though he knew it was a mistake. 'Why? Don't you think we can?'

'I don't know. I want to, but…'

She tailed off and Ewan realised that whatever he did next was going to determine which direction their relationship took. His head began to spin as thoughts raced this way and that. Did he want them to be solely friends or did he want them to be more than that? Could he face the thought of falling in love with her again after what had happened the last time? On the other hand, was he strong enough to stop it happening?

It felt as though a lifetime had passed while

he churned it all over in his head, but in truth it was mere seconds. For every question there was an answer, the same answer repeated time after time: Yes. Yes. Yes! He was already reaching for her before the last yes faded, already sure that he was doing the right thing. He wanted her so much, wanted to be her friend, her lover, plus everything beyond and in between.

Their mouths met and it was as though they had never been apart. It was like finding a part of himself that had been missing, Ewan realised in wonder. He may have kissed a lot of women since he'd last kissed Becky but not one of them had made this impact on him. When they finally broke apart, he could tell that Becky was as stunned by what had happened as he was. She hadn't expected this reaction either and now it was up to him to ensure that she didn't end up feeling guilty.

'Wow! That was some kiss,' he said, adopting a deliberately teasing tone.

'I...erm...yes, it was,' she agreed huskily.

Ewan felt the tiny hairs all over his body stand to attention. Had she any idea how deliciously

sexy she sounded? he wondered, before he ruth-
lessly erased the thought. He mustn't get too
far ahead of himself, mustn't try to lead her
down a path she might not want to take. Maybe
Becky had enjoyed the kiss but it didn't mean
she wanted to make love with him.

. He took her hand, overwhelmed by a sudden
need to protect her. Making love with her was
what he wanted—desperately!—but his needs
had to come second to hers. 'It seems that the
old feelings aren't dead after all. The question
is where do we go from here? If we stop now,
we may still be able to remain friends, but if we
move things up a notch, that won't be possible.'

'I realise that.' She looked into his eyes and
he could see the uncertainty in hers. 'I don't
know, Ewan—that's the honest answer. Part of
me knows it would be wrong to pick up where
we left off but the other part…'

She shrugged, leaving him to fill in the rest,
which he did with alacrity. Bending, he kissed
her again, just lightly and with infinite tenderness. 'I feel the same, Becky. Part of me feels it

would be madness if we got involved, but another part can't think of anything I want more.'

'Then maybe we should take time to think about it,' she suggested.

She looked at him and Ewan felt his breath catch when he saw the desire in her eyes. It was all he could do not to haul her back into his arms and kiss her until neither of them could think straight, but he had to be sensible, had to make sure it was what they both truly wanted. There was too much at stake and it would be far too easy to end up getting hurt.

'I think it's a good idea,' he said quietly, feeling the first stirrings of alarm. When they had decided against getting involved before, he had felt hurt but not devastated. His feelings had been tempered by relief because his plans to travel wouldn't need to be changed, but it was different now. Something warned him that it would be far worse to lose Becky this time round. 'We don't want to rush into anything and regret it, do we?'

'No, we don't.' Her fingers closed around his. 'The last thing I want is either of us getting hurt, Ewan.'

'I don't want that either.' He squeezed her hand then glanced round when he heard the back door opening. 'It sounds as though your parents are home.' He stood up, not wanting to cause her any embarrassment by having Ros and Simon find them in such a compromising position. 'I'd better go. I'm due in work early tomorrow but I'll phone you in the evening, if that's okay?'

'Fine.'

She stood up as well, smoothing down her dress. Ewan turned and ran down the stairs, trying not to think about how he would have loved to help her out of it. He could just imagine inching down the zip a fraction at a time while he laid a trail of kisses down her spine....

'Ah, just off, are you, Ewan?' Simon appeared from the direction of the kitchen and Ewan hastily rid himself of such tantalising thoughts.

'Yes. I'm in work early tomorrow,' he explained, glancing round when Becky appeared. Heat roared through his veins as the image of her standing in front of him, half-naked, came flooding back. Her skin would be so soft and so smooth, like the finest satin. He could imagine how it would feel beneath his hands and his lips....

'No rest for the wicked, eh?' Simon said cheerfully.

Ewan started, afraid that he'd said something revealing before he realised that Simon was referring to his early start. 'So they say,' he agreed with as much aplomb as he could muster. 'Right, I'll be off then. I'll speak to you tomorrow, Becky.'

'Fine.'

She gave him a quick smile and he couldn't help feeling disappointed even though he knew it was ridiculous to expect anything more with her father standing there. He said goodnight to Ros on his way out and walked back to The Ship Inn to collect his car, calling himself a whole load of unflattering names.

He was an idiot if he imagined that Becky was going to declare her feelings for him in front of her parents! If truth be told, she wasn't sure how she felt and neither was he. Oh, that kiss had been magical; there was no doubt about that. However, it didn't prove she loved him now any more than it had proved she'd loved him eight years ago.

Ewan slammed the car door, aware that he was doing the one thing he had sworn he wouldn't do. He was on the verge of falling in love with Becky all over again.

CHAPTER ELEVEN

'THIS IS THE last time you'll need to come in to the surgery, Mrs Rose. Your leg has healed beautifully and it won't need dressing anymore.'

Becky smiled at the old lady, doing her best to set aside her own problems, but it wasn't easy. She'd spent the night thinking about her and Ewan and what she should do. Would it be right to have a relationship with him when she knew it couldn't lead anywhere? Her head said no but her heart said just the opposite. If her heart had its way then she and Ewan would be the couple everyone believed them to be very soon.

She cleared her throat, trying not to think about all that it entailed. Thinking about making love with Ewan certainly wouldn't help her reach a measured decision. 'You'll need to be careful, of course. The new skin is still very delicate and you don't want to damage it. But all things considered, you've done remarkably well.'

'That's good to hear, my dear.' Mrs Rose beamed at her. 'It's all down to your excellent care, of course. I really appreciate the trouble you've taken.'

'It's been no trouble,' Becky declared truthfully. She put the soiled dressing into the hazardous waste bin and peeled off her gloves, popping them in as well. 'You've been a model patient. I only wish there were more people like you.'

Mrs Rose laughed. 'Some folk can be a little troublesome, I imagine. I must confess that I'm not looking forward to taking care of my son once he's discharged from hospital. Geoffrey isn't what you would call an easy person to help.'

'I didn't know your son was ill!' Becky exclaimed. 'I'm so sorry.'

'Oh, it was his own fault. He was the driver of the car that collided with that coach at the weekend.' Mrs Rose looked disapproving. 'It appears he was using his mobile phone at the time. Geoffrey has denied it, of course, but the police have applied for a copy of his phone records and no doubt they will prove he was on the phone at the time.'

'Oh, dear.' Becky grimaced. 'It sounds as though he may be charged with dangerous driving.'

'It will serve him right,' Mrs Rose said sternly. 'It's only by the grace of God that no one was killed.'

Becky nodded, knowing it was true. She added a note to Mrs Rose's file to the effect that she was discharging her and smiled. 'That's it, then. I shall miss our little chats now that you won't need to pop in to see me.'

'So will I.' Mrs Rose sighed as she stood up. 'It gets rather lonely, living on your own, especially since Emily moved away.'

'Oh, so you and Emily were friends, were you?' Becky asked, not wanting to hurry the old lady after what she'd said.

'Friends and neighbours, actually. Emily rented the cottage next to mine and I really miss not having her and little Theo around.' Mrs Rose shook her head. 'The agents are thinking of letting it out as a holiday rental but it won't be the same. I mean, you can't get to know people if they're only there for a couple of weeks.'

'Would they consider another long-term let?' Becky asked slowly, wondering if this might be the answer to her problems. If she could afford the rent then she and Millie would have a home of their own again.

'Oh, yes. They'd prefer it, in fact. Why? Are you interested in renting it, my dear?' Mrs Rose had perked up at the thought.

Becky nodded. 'Yes, I am. My parents have been marvellous but I really would like to find a place of our own for me and Millie.'

'The cottage would be ideal!' Mrs Rose assured her. 'Emily got it looking really nice inside. And although the garden is small, it's all fenced in so you wouldn't have to worry about your little girl getting out.'

'It sounds perfect.'

Becky wrote down the details of the agents who were handling the property then saw Mrs Rose out. She went back to her room, buoyed up by the thought of having a home of her own again. Much as she loved her parents, it was what she wanted, to be independent while she raised Millie. Maybe it hadn't been her goal a few years ago but things had changed since then. She was never going to be a happily married mum, looking after her brood, but a single parent with a child to raise. She frowned. Maybe she should make sure that Ewan understood that before they went any further?

'You look shattered. What did you get up to at the weekend, or shouldn't I ask?'

Ewan grinned when Cathy Morrison accosted him in the staffroom. 'Oh, you can ask all right, although you'll be disappointed by the answer. I ended up helping out at that coach crash. It kind of ruined my peaceful day off.'

'Really?' Cathy grimaced as she switched on the kettle. 'I'd say that was above and beyond the call of duty. What did you do—follow the ambulances to see where they were going?'

'No way!' Ewan laughed. 'I gave up ambulance chasing a while back. I leave that to the insurance people these days. No, I just happened to be around when the call came through and went along to help. A couple of doctors from Bride's Bay Surgery were having a party and they invited me along,' he added by way of explanation.

'Oh, hard luck. Still, it'll teach you to hob-nob with other medics during off-duty hours.' Cathy grinned as she spooned instant coffee into a couple of mugs. 'You should do what I do and make sure that all your friends are strictly non-medical!'

'I shall bear it in mind,' Ewan agreed with a grin as he accepted the mug of coffee.

Cathy took her coffee back to the desk, leaving him alone with his thoughts. He sighed as he sank down onto a chair. The call-out was only partially to blame for his weariness. The real culprit was lack of sleep. He'd spent the night tossing and turning while the same thought had whizzed around his head: was he completely mad to consider getting involved with Becky?

A week ago—less, even—he would have agreed wholeheartedly with that sentiment but not any longer. The thought of a future without Becky was impossible to imagine and that's what worried him most of all. He had gone from not wanting to get involved with her to needing to know she would be part of his life in what seemed like the blink of an eye. If that wasn't a sign he was crazy then heaven knew what was!

Ewan got up and tipped the rest of the coffee down the sink. He couldn't bear to sit there, churning it all over again. He went back to the unit, lifting the next patient's notes out of the tray. It would be better if he kept himself busy, although he would have to decide what he was going to do soon. Becky was expecting him to phone her that night and he needed to know what tone the call should take. Light and friendly? Or something deeper?

He grimaced. He knew what he really wanted to do, but it didn't mean it was right.

It was almost eight before the telephone rang. Becky shot to her feet, smiling sheepishly when her mother looked at her in surprise. 'I'd better get that before it wakes Millie,' she said, hurrying out of the room.

Snatching up the receiver, she pressed it to her ear, wondering why she felt so nervous. It was just a phone call. Nothing to get excited about. However, the fact that it might be Ewan phoning gave it a whole new significance. 'Dr Harper's residence. Becky speaking.'

'Becky, it's Ewan. Hi!'

He sounded so light and breezy, a world away from the nervous wreck she'd turned into, that Becky couldn't help feeling a little irritated. 'Oh, hello, Ewan. I'd forgotten you said you'd ring tonight. How are you?'

'Tired but that's nothing new.' He gave a short laugh and she heard the edge it held. He obviously hadn't appreciated her comment but hard luck. While she'd been worrying herself to death, he'd been swanning about without a care in the world, apparently. She hardened her heart. 'Are you phoning about something special or just for a chat?'

'Both, actually. But if you're busy, it will keep until another time. Enjoy your evening.'

'Wait!' Becky realised that he was going to hang up and knew that she couldn't bear to be left wondering. She needed to know what he had decided, come what may. 'I'm not doing anything important,' she admitted, swallowing her pride.

'Well, if you're sure...' There was a hint, the merest trace of laughter in his voice, and she glared at the receiver even though he couldn't possibly see her.

'Of course I'm sure!'

'Good.' His voice softened, flowing down the line like warm honey, and her irritation melted away. 'I've been thinking about you all day. That's why I was so late in calling you. I couldn't decide what I was going to say.'

'I understand.' She sighed. 'It isn't easy, is it? I mean, we didn't expect this to happen, did we?'

'No. If I'm honest it was the last thing I wanted but I won't lie to you, Becky. I still have feelings for you and I think you still have them for me, too.'

'I do.' She bit her lip, unwilling to say anything else. They were still on fairly safe ground at the moment, still able to step back, but once they moved their relationship onto a physical level that wouldn't be possible. The thought made her shudder with sudden apprehension.

'So what are we going to do?' he said softly. 'I may as well admit that I still haven't made up my mind. Have you?'

'No. Part of me wants us to remain friends because it would be so much simpler that way…'

'And another part wants us to be more than friends,' he said, finishing the sentence. 'It's the same for me, if it's any consolation.'

'So what do you suggest?'

'I suppose the sensible thing is to take it slowly and not rush into anything. At the moment we're still in shock and it would be stupid to let ourselves get carried away. Maybe in a week or so's time we'll have a clearer idea of what we want.'

'That sounds like a good idea to me.'

'Does it?' He laughed. 'Miracle of miracles. I'm actually making sense even though it feels as though my head is spinning!'

Becky laughed as well. 'Mine too. So how do you want to play this? Shall we see one another, purely on a friendly basis, of course?'

'I don't think we'll ever work this out if we don't,' he said wryly. 'I'm on earlies all week but I'm off on Saturday so do you fancy doing something then, maybe take Millie to the beach if the weather's fine?'

'That would be lovely…oh, the thing is, I've arranged to view a cottage on Saturday morning. Emily used to live there and it sounds ideal.'

'I'll come with you,' he offered at once and she laughed.

'Would you? That would be great.'

They arranged what time he would pick her and Millie up before they hung up. Becky went back to the sitting room, hoping that she hadn't made a mistake. She didn't want to hurt Ewan but there was no guarantee it wouldn't happen if they got close again. At the end of the day she mustn't forget that she could never give Ewan the family he would want one day.

'Who was that, darling?' Ros looked up as she went back into the room and Becky did her best to put on a cheerful face.

'Ewan. We've arranged to meet on Saturday.' Becky took a quick breath, deciding that it would be better to get it all over with in one fell swoop. She'd been trying to work out the best way to broach the subject but there was really only one way. 'Actually, I'm going to look at a house that's for rent. It's Emily's old home and it sounds perfect for me and Millie.'

'I thought you'd want to find a place of your own once you got settled,' Ros said calmly.

'You don't mind? Don't think I'm ungrateful, will you? You and Dad have been marvellous but it would be good to have my own space,' Becky explained anxiously.

'I understand, darling. Really I do.' Ros smiled at her. 'You're a grown woman with a child of your own—it would be strange if you didn't want your own home.'

'Thank you.' Becky went and gave her mother a hug.

'There's nothing to thank me for. Your father and I only want what's best for you.' Ros frowned. 'Are you sure you know what you're doing with regard to Ewan, though? Don't get me wrong, I'd be over the moon if you two got together but I got the impression that it was never going to happen.'

'It isn't. I like Ewan, more than just like him, if I'm honest. But I won't ruin his life, Mum.'

'He may not see it like that,' Ros pointed out.

'Maybe not but it's a risk I'm not willing to take.' Becky shrugged. 'Ewan needs someone who can give him a family eventually. And that's something I can't do.'

'I'm so sorry, darling.'

Becky smiled sadly. 'Me too.'

Ros changed the subject. She obviously didn't want to upset her, although Becky knew that talking about the issue wouldn't make it any worse. She couldn't have another child and that was final. No amount of discussion would solve the problem, although it didn't mean she intended to tell Ewan. Knowing Ewan, he would probably claim it didn't matter but she knew that it did. She had no intention of ruining his chances of having a family of his own one day.

Saturday dawned bright and clear. Ewan was up before six despite the fact that he and Becky weren't due to meet until mid-morning. He took a shower, whistling to himself as the water pounded down on his head. He felt all bright-eyed and bushy-tailed and it was all down to

Becky. The thought of spending the day with her was a definite boost to his spirits. How marvellous it would be if he could spend the rest of his life with her.

The thought stayed with him while he ate his breakfast. The main reason he had come back to England was to settle down. Although he had enjoyed seeing something of the world and wouldn't have missed it for anything, he had realised recently that he wanted more. It was time to put down roots, find the woman he wanted to spend his life with and start a family. Now that he'd met Becky again, it seemed that all the boxes had been ticked. He couldn't think of anything better than having Becky as his wife and the mother of his children.

Ewan put his dishes in the sink and picked up his car keys. Even though it was way too early to set off, he needed to see Becky and find out if she felt the same as him. Maybe they had agreed to take things slowly but he couldn't bear the thought of waiting. He needed to know if there was a chance that Becky loved him!

* * *

Becky had just finished getting Millie dressed when she heard a car pull up. Hurrying to the window, she gasped when she saw Ewan getting out. What on earth was he doing here at this time of the morning? She ran downstairs to let him in.

'I know, I know. I'm horribly early.' He grinned at her, his blue eyes alight with laughter and something else, something that made her pulse race. 'I'll understand if you tell me to take a hike.'

'Of course not.' Becky dredged up a smile but her heart was pounding away as though it was trying for a new world record. To have Ewan look at her with all that desire in his eyes wasn't easy to deal with. She cleared her throat. 'Mum and Dad are still in bed but Millie's up. Go on through to the kitchen while I fetch her.'

She ran back upstairs and picked Millie up then paused while she tried to calm herself down. She had to remember that they were taking things slowly....

Ewan didn't seem to be setting too much store by that idea, though, did he?

Becky shook her head to dislodge that insidious thought and carried Millie downstairs. Ewan had the kettle on and he looked round when she went in.

'Tea or coffee?'

'Tea, please.' Becky popped Millie into her highchair. Although the little girl had already eaten her breakfast, she peeled a banana and gave it to her, then sat down.

'Here you go.' Ewan placed a mug in front of her. Bending over, he pretended to take a bite of Millie's banana. 'Yummy, scrummy. That looks delicious.'

Millie chuckled as she tried to ram the fruit into his mouth and he laughed. Taking a handkerchief out of his pocket, he wiped away the mashed banana smeared all round his mouth. 'Thank you, sweetheart. It's really kind of you to give me a taste.'

Becky sighed as she watched the interplay between them. Ewan was so good with Millie, seeming to know exactly how to treat her. He had a natural affinity with children and would make the most wonderful father. Pain ripped through her and she glanced down at her tea, not wanting him to suspect anything was wrong. She had made up her mind that she wasn't going to tell Ewan about her not being able to have any more children and she must stick to it.

'So what time are you meeting the agents?'

She looked up when he spoke, adopting a deliberately upbeat tone. 'Ten-thirty.'

'Have you told your parents what you're planning?' he asked, pulling out a chair. He was wearing fawn chinos and Becky felt her pulse race even faster as she saw the fabric tauten across his muscular thighs.

'Yes, and they're fine about it,' she said huskily. 'They understand that I need my own space.'

'I didn't think it would be a problem.' He grinned at her. 'Fingers crossed that the cottage turns out to be suitable.'

'Ditto.' Becky made a great production of crossing her fingers. She had to be sensible, had to remember that no matter how much she wanted Ewan, they didn't have a future together. She stood up, unable to deal with the thought right then. 'I'll make a start on our picnic. Cheese and ham sandwiches all right with you?'

'Perfect.' He captured her hand as she came around the table. 'I've been looking forward to today, Becky.'

'Me too.'

She gave him a quick smile before she freed herself. Taking the bread out of the bread bin, she set to work and in a very short time had assembled their picnic. It was easier when she had something to do, less stressful. When Ewan offered his help, she declined, deeming it safer to leave him sitting in the chair rather than run the risk of them bumping into one another.

She gulped because she knew where that would lead. The thought of making love with Ewan both scared and thrilled her. Their relationship had never reached that point eight years ago; she had broken it off before they had got that far. However, she knew that once it happened, it would be even harder to do the right thing. And the right thing meant walking away. Again.

CHAPTER TWELVE

THE COTTAGE WAS perfect. Ewan could tell that Becky was going to take it even before the agent had finished showing them round. Once everything was agreed and the agent had left, they took a last look around the garden. Becky couldn't hide her delight as she lifted Millie onto a junior-sized swing that Emily had left behind.

'This is going to be our new home, sweetheart. You'll love living here, won't you?'

Ewan laughed. 'I'm not sure Millie understands you.'

'Of course she does! She's a very intelligent little girl—can't you tell?'

'Oh, I can.' He smiled back, relieved that she seemed to have got over whatever had been troubling her earlier. He'd had the distinct impression when they were in the kitchen that she'd been keeping her distance, although he wasn't

sure why. 'She's very like her mother in that respect,' he declared, deciding not to say anything.
It was only natural that Becky should have reservations about them, after all.

'I shall take that as a compliment, thank you.'
Becky lifted Millie off the swing, shaking her
head when she started to wail. 'We have to go
now, darling, but we can come back again very
soon.'

Millie refused to be mollified, however. She
screamed even louder as they made their way
down the path. Ewan bent and looked into her
angry little face.

'What a racket! You're making so much noise
that you're frightening the birds.'

Millie stopped screaming and looked at him in
surprise. He took her from Becky, holding her
up so she could see the flock of sparrows nesting
in the bushes that ran alongside the path. 'See,
there they are. If you keep very quiet you'll hear
them singing.'

Mille stared at them in wide-eyed wonder and
Becky laughed. 'You seem to be a dab hand at

this. How come you know so much about entertaining young children?'

'One of the benefits of being an uncle to so many little nieces and nephews,' he replied wryly. 'You have to find ways to distract them if you hope to survive!'

'Really?' Becky frowned. 'But surely you haven't seen that much of your family with working abroad?'

'More than you'd think.' He swung Millie onto his shoulders and gave her a piggyback to the car. 'Anna lives in France so I spent a lot of time with her and her family while I was working there. And Fiona has moved to Spain—Marbella, which is a great place for holidays as I discovered. Then there's Shona—I think I told you that I stayed with her on my way back here.'

'You did. You said she was expecting another child—has she had it yet?'

'Yes. Another little girl.' He grinned as he unlocked the car. 'Ryan's girlfriend is expecting too so I'll have to get a move on if I hope to compete with the rest of my family!'

'You certainly will.'

Becky gave him a quick smile but Ewan was aware that some of the sparkle had gone out of it. What had he said? he wondered as he handed Millie over so Becky could strap her into her seat. He had no idea but it seemed that he had touched a nerve.

He drove them straight to Pringle's Cove after they left the cottage. Although the beach there was much smaller than the one at nearby Denton's Cove, there were lots of rock pools, which he knew Millie would enjoy exploring. Drawing up close to the top of the footpath, he switched off the engine.

'I'll fetch our bits and bobs while you carry Millie.'

'Are you sure you can manage?' Becky asked as she got out of the car. She looked dubiously into the boot. 'We seem to have an awful lot of stuff in there.'

'I'll just bring the essentials for now and come back for the rest as and when it's needed,' he assured her.

'Oh, right. Good idea.'

She set off down the path while Ewan gathered

together what they needed. The picnic basket and the rug were essentials, as were a child-sized bucket and spade. He piled everything on the ground then reached for the parasol he'd discovered at the back of a cupboard, stopping when he heard a scream from below. Hurrying to the top of the path, he peered down, his heart turning over when he saw Becky lying sprawled on the ground. He ran down to her, skidding to a halt when he reached her.

'Are you all right?'

'I think so.' She went to stand up, no easy task when she still had hold of Millie.

'Let me take her.' Ewan took the little girl off her, putting his hand under Becky's elbow as he helped her to her feet.

'Thanks. My foot caught on a stone and down I went. Is Millie all right?' she asked anxiously.

'She's fine, aren't you, poppet?' Ewan gave the child a cuddle then took a firmer grip on Becky's arm. 'Let's get you down safely before I go back for our things.'

Becky didn't protest as he helped her down the rest of the path. Ewan guessed that the fall had shaken her up but he didn't say anything. Becky wouldn't appreciate him fussing over her. She wasn't the sort of woman who demanded attention, although maybe he should have paid her more attention eight years ago and then she might not have married Steve. He sighed as he left her and Millie sitting on a piece of driftwood and went back for their things. It was pointless thinking like that. Becky had married Steve and nothing would change that fact. All he could do was hope that she would get over losing her husband in time.

Despite its inauspicious start, the afternoon turned out perfectly. Ewan was patience itself as he helped Millie make dozens of sand pies. He even dug a trench so the sea could form a moat around them, much to Millie's delight. As Becky listened to her daughter's squeals of joy as the water flowed along the channel, she couldn't help feeling sad. If things had been different then Millie could have been the luckiest little girl in the world. She could have had Ewan around to love and care for her while she was growing up.

'I...am...pooped!' Ewan deposited a decidedly sandy Millie onto the rug and flopped down beside her. 'This little lady has worn me out.'

'I thought you said you were an expert at looking after little ones,' Becky retorted, determined not to let him know how she was feeling. She knew the score, understood that Ewan could never take on the role of Millie's father, and there was no point torturing herself.

'Hmm, obviously I had a rather rosy view of my prowess.' He raked back his hair and grinned wickedly at her. 'Remind me not to make any false claims in the future, will you?'

Even though ostensibly they were discussing his claim to be an expert childminder, Becky blushed. She busied herself with unpacking the picnic, trying not to think about what else Ewan might claim to be an expert at. So what if he was a wonderful lover? There was no guarantee that they were compatible, was there?

The thought nagged away at her as they ate. She had lost all interest in sex in recent years and it was worrying to wonder how she would react if she and Ewan made love, especially in view of what Steve had said. She couldn't bear to think that he had been right and that she was frigid.

Millie fell asleep as soon as she had finished her lunch. Becky laid her down on the rug, frowning as she looked round for something to use as a sunshade. The sun was quite strong now and she didn't want Millie getting burnt.

'Use this.' Ewan produced a battered-looking parasol. He dug it into the sand, angling it so that Millie was sheltered from the sun's rays.

'That's great. Where on earth did you get it, though?'

'I found it in the back of a cupboard. The previous tenants must have left it behind when they moved out of the flat.' Ewan sat down again, resting his forearms across his up-bent knees as he stared out to sea. 'It's so peaceful here. It's hard to believe that only a few miles away there are people rushing about.'

'It must make a pleasant change after working in ED all week,' Becky observed, leaning back on her elbows. She tilted her face to the sun, enjoying its warmth. It seemed ages since she'd had time to relax like this and she intended to make the most of it.

'True. Although, I must admit that I love the job.' He shrugged. 'I must be a bit of masochist, I suppose.'

'You always wanted to work in emergency medicine,' she pointed out, turning to look at him.

'I did.' He smiled at her. 'I guess I'm one of the lucky ones. Not everyone gets to do a job they love. Oh, that reminds me, did I tell you that I called in to see Sandra Fielding?'

'The lady who fractured her femur in the coach crash?'

'That's the one. She's doing very well, you'll be glad to hear, although whether that's down to the excellent nursing care she's received or because her friend—Edward, isn't it?—cancelled his flight home to Canada so he could be with her, I'm not sure.' He laughed. 'They say that love is the best medicine of all and they could be right.'

'Really? Oh, how lovely!' Becky exclaimed.

'Isn't it?' His voice dropped, sounding deeper

than ever, and she shivered. 'I think it proves that time doesn't always destroy people's feelings.'

He leant sideways and Becky knew that he was going to kiss her. Just for a moment panic assailed her as she wondered if it was right to let their relationship take this direction. But then Ewan's lips found hers and all her doubts fled. She wanted his kiss, wanted it so much that she couldn't bear to wait another second.

Their mouths met with a small jolt and she heard him sigh, knew that he understood how desperate she felt because he felt the same. Ewan was as eager for this kiss as she was. Their mouths clung then parted. Becky closed her eyes when she felt his lips skim over her face, scattering butterfly-soft kisses along the way. She could feel the sun on her skin, see its glow through her closed eyelids, and it felt as though she was suddenly enveloped in warmth and light. Ewan's mouth was so hot, his lips burning as they travelled over her skin. Everywhere they touched it felt as though a flame had ignited. Would it always be this way? she wondered dizzily. Or would her delight in his kisses fade with time?

'I didn't think it could ever be as good between us as it was before.' Ewan drew back and Becky shuddered when she saw the desire in his eyes.

'And is it?' she asked huskily.

'No.' He dropped a kiss on her mouth, letting his lips linger, and she knew it was because he couldn't bear to break the contact. When he finally pulled away his face was set, the tense line of his jaw hinting at the struggle he'd had. 'It's even better.'

He eased her down onto the rug and kissed her again, his mouth demanding a response that she was more than willing to give. Becky could feel desire roaring through her veins, feel her blood heating and her heart racing. Ewan was right, she thought, it was better now: more passionate, more sensual, more...*everything*!

They were both breathless when they broke apart, both trembling as though they had a fever. Becky could feel little flurries of heat rippling beneath her skin and knew they had nothing to do with the weather. It was Ewan who had set her alight; his kisses had reawoken her passion and proved that she wasn't frigid.

'Although I hate to say this, we should stop.' He ran his thumb over her swollen lips and she felt him shudder and shuddered too. He had to breathe in and out before he could continue. 'It's not exactly private here, is it? I'd hate it if someone came along and found us in what could only be called a compromising position.'

Becky blushed as her mind conjured up the scene. The thought of making love with Ewan right here on the beach was so tempting but she knew he was right to call a halt. Even if they had the cove to themselves there was Millie to consider: she could wake up at any moment.

'You're right. I'd hate it too. It would make it seem so cheap and tawdry...'

'Which it isn't.' He kissed her softly and with infinite tenderness. 'There's nothing cheap or tawdry about what we're doing, Becky.'

'I know that.'

'Good. I'd hate to think that you felt it was wrong in any way.'

She saw the question in his eyes and shook her head. 'I don't think that, Ewan. Really, I don't.'

'So long as you're sure it's what you want?' He

gave her a moment to reconsider then shrugged. 'At least we're clear on that point. Now we have to decide how to handle this. I understand if you don't want to go public so maybe we should keep this to ourselves until you're comfortable with the idea of us being a couple.'

'I don't think we need to worry unduly about that,' she said, her heart sinking. She took a quick breath but she had to make it clear that no matter what happened, they weren't going down the happily-ever-after route. It would be wrong to mislead him, wrong and cruel to offer him something she couldn't deliver. 'I imagine folk will get the message eventually. Once the expected announcements—engagement, wedding—don't materialise, they'll give up.'

'I'm sure they will.'

Ewan's tone was bland. If he was upset by what she'd said, it didn't show. Becky couldn't help feeling hurt even though she knew how selfish it was. She should be glad that he didn't consider their relationship to be a long-term arrangement. At least this way he wouldn't get hurt.

Hc stood up, brushing the sand off his legs, and she forced herself to smile even though it felt as though her heart had split wide open. 'So we're agreed, then. We shall be discreet and leave everyone to watch and wonder.'

'Sounds good to me.' He glanced towards the sea, shading his eyes against the glare so that it was impossible to read his expression. 'Right, I think I'll go for a swim. With a bit of luck the sun will have taken some of the chill off the water by now.'

He stripped off his T-shirt and dropped it onto the sand. His trousers quickly followed, leaving him clad only in a pair of black swimming shorts. Becky gulped as she was treated to a glimpse of his hard, tanned body before he jogged towards the water. He plunged into the waves, swimming strongly towards the mouth of the bay.

Becky watched him until her eyes blurred, until she was unable to distinguish the sea from the sky. Lying back on the rug, she tried to console herself with the thought that she had done the right thing, but it didn't help. She might want

Ewan even though she knew she couldn't have him, but it was obvious that he didn't want her. Oh, he might be happy to have a relationship with her, would certainly enjoy making love to her, but he didn't see her as part of his future. It made her wonder if he had his own agenda for taking up with her. Was he trying to get even with her for the way she had rejected him? It was possible. Anything was possible. Ewan could be playing her for a fool....

Only she didn't really believe that, did she? It wasn't Ewan's way to be deceitful. He was far too honest to play those sorts of games. Which meant that she'd been right in the first place. Ewan considered her to be a temporary addition to his life, a pleasant distraction. Nothing more and nothing less.

Ewan swam until his lungs burned and his arms felt as though they had turned to lead. Rolling over onto his back, he let the waves carry him back towards the shore. It was lucky the tide was coming in as he doubted he had the strength to get back there under his own steam.

He swore roundly, cursing his own stupidity and the fact that he had allowed his emotions to strip away his common sense. So what if Becky didn't want to spend her life with him? It was hardly a surprise. She'd had her chance eight years ago and decided against it. It wasn't as though he had spent those years pining for her either. He'd had a lot of fun, lived life to the fullest, and enjoyed himself both with and without a female companion in tow. Maybe Becky did seem to press an awful lot of buttons but he would meet someone else who pressed even more. The law of averages made that a certainty. Out of all the women in all the world, Becky couldn't be the only one he'd fall in love with…

Could she?

Ewan ditched that thought before it could grow wings. Rolling over, he forced his tired limbs into a rapid crawl that soon had him back at the beach. He stood up and shook himself, watching the droplets of water leave pockmarks in the smooth damp sand. Not so long ago it had felt as though everything he had ever wished for was within his reach but now that idea was pockmarked with doubts, like the sand under his feet. Becky might be happy to have a relationship with him but she was never going to make a lifetime's commitment to them as a couple.

Millie was awake when he went back. He towelled himself dry and dragged on his clothes. Becky had packed up the remains of their picnic and he took it as a sign that she was ready to leave. Maybe she'd realised that they'd had the best out of the day and that it was all downhill from this point on.

The thought was depressing. It was an effort to appear upbeat as he picked up Millie. 'I'll carry Millie up the path. I wouldn't want you to slip again.'

'Thanks.'

Becky sounded unusually subdued but he refused to speculate about the reason for it. If she didn't want to share her life with him then she definitely wouldn't want to share her thoughts. He set off up the path, singing a rousing version of 'Baa Baa Black Sheep' to amuse Millie as well as distract himself. There were too many dark thoughts whizzing around his head, thoughts he wouldn't want to share with Becky either. He sighed. Maybe they were equally at fault. He was just as determined to keep his counsel as she was hers, it seemed.

He handed Millie over then went back to collect their things. By the time he had stowed everything in the boot, the sun had disappeared behind a bank of ominously black clouds. He grimaced as he started the engine.

'Looks like we're leaving at the right time. There's a storm brewing.'

The words were barely out of his mouth when the first raindrops fell from the sky. Ewan turned on the windscreen wipers as he looked for somewhere to turn the car around. The lane leading to Pringle's Cove was extremely narrow, which was one of the reasons why very few visitors made it there. It also made reversing a problem.

'There's a gateway further down the road. You should be able to turn round there,' Becky suggested, leaning forward to point through the windscreen.

Ewan flinched when her arm brushed against his. He gritted his teeth as he drove towards where she'd indicated. He needed to reassess the situation, decide what he wanted to do and not simply be led by his emotions. He turned the car around and headed back to Bride's Bay. What it all came down to was simple: could he handle having a relationship with Becky that was based on sex and nothing more?

CHAPTER THIRTEEN

A WEEK PASSED, then a second, and still Becky didn't hear a word from Ewan. She found herself lingering by the telephone each evening like a lovesick teenager but couldn't help it. She missed him. Missed hearing his voice, missed seeing his smile, just missed him. In a few short weeks he had become an important part of her life and every day she didn't see or speak to him felt emptier because of it.

She knew that at some point she would have to face up to the reason why she felt this way, but not just yet. It was too much, too soon; she wasn't ready. She couldn't handle the fact, either, that no matter how she felt, she could never tell Ewan. She had to protect him even though it appeared he might not need protecting after all. Ewan's feelings seemed to be far more prosaic than hers were.

The start of the new month loomed and Becky got ready to move into the cottage. Her parents had been typically generous and insisted on buying her some furniture. She had sold her old furniture before she'd come back to England, not wanting it as a reminder of her former life. She would have had next to nothing to furnish her new home if her parents hadn't bought her a table and chairs, a bed and a sofa as well as giving her the new nursery furniture, and Becky was suitably grateful.

Thankfully, it was a dry day when she moved in. Her father had hired a van and Tom and Hannah had offered their help as well. Her mother had insisted on looking after Millie and Charlie so the four of them were able to concentrate on getting everything sorted out. By six o'clock that evening, the house was ready.

'I can't believe we've got everything done!' Becky exclaimed, looking around the sitting room. The new sofa with its pale green covers and heap of colourful cushions looked even better than she'd hoped and she smiled in delight.

'It looks absolutely lovely in here. Thank you all so much. You've been brilliant.'

'Our pleasure.' Hannah gave her a hug. 'I take it that Ewan was working today and that's why he couldn't be here to help?'

'I…erm…that's right.' Becky knew it was silly but she simply couldn't bring herself to admit that she hadn't seen Ewan in weeks. Hannah would want to know why and she couldn't face the thought of having to explain the situation to her.

'He probably volunteered to work overtime so he could avoid it,' Tom observed cheerfully. He glanced at his watch, mercifully sparing Becky from having to reply. 'We're going to have to cut and run, I'm afraid. Charlie's usually in bed by seven and it's better if we don't upset his routine.' He kissed Becky's cheek. 'I hope you'll be very happy here, Becky. You deserve to be.'

Becky felt tears rush to her eyes. 'Thanks, Tom.'

She kissed Hannah and her father and thanked them again then went back to the sitting room and sat down. Millie was spending the night with her parents as Becky had decided it would be less unsettling for her if the house was ready when Millie moved in. She hadn't expected to get everything finished so quickly and now the evening stretched before her. She wasn't sure what she was going to do with the time. The only thing left was to make herself some supper and watch television.

Becky went into the kitchen and set to work, cutting up some chicken for a stir-fry even though she really wasn't hungry. Still, it stopped her thinking about Ewan and the fact that he obviously didn't care a jot about her. How could he do when he hadn't even bothered to phone and wish her well?

Her knife flew as she chopped a mound of vegetables. There was far too much for one person but so what? What did an extra bit of broccoli matter in the great scheme of things? The man she loved didn't love her—that was what mattered.

It was only when that thought sank in that Becky stopped what she was doing. She loved Ewan. It wasn't a question but a statement. She loved him. How it had happened she had no idea but she had fallen in love with him all over again, always assuming that she had fallen out of love with him in the first place, and she was no longer sure about that. She had opted for security, for the kind of life she had dreamed of having when she had chosen to stay with Steve, but she had never loved him the way she loved Ewan. Her love for Ewan would last a lifetime—her lifetime, not his.

Ewan stopped the car and switched off the engine. Night was falling and the light from the cottage cast a puddle of yellow across the path. He had spent the day wrestling with himself and lost. He knew it was a mistake to come here but he had to see Becky even if it was only to wish her well. Reaching over to the back seat, he picked up the bouquet he'd bought that afternoon. He'd opted for gerberas rather than roses because roses could have given out the wrong message. He was a friend wishing her well in her new home, not a lover come to court her.

His footsteps rang as hollowly as his thoughts

as he walked up the path. He knocked on the door, just one light rap of his knuckles on the wood so that he wouldn't wake Millie. He could hear movements inside and imagined Becky getting up, wondering who it was, wondering if she should answer. Would she be more inclined to open the door if she knew it was him or less? He had no idea.

The door opened and there she was. Ewan felt his heart swell, felt it fill with so many emotions that he couldn't speak. He had missed her so much. Missed her more than he'd believed it possible to miss anyone. And it was then that it hit him that he loved her. Then when he felt at his most vulnerable. He loved her and there was nothing he could do about it, the same as there was nothing he could about the fact that she didn't love him.

'Ewan!'

He heard the surprise in her voice and rallied. Holding out the bouquet, he smiled at her. 'I brought you these to welcome you to your new home.'

'Thank you. They're lovely.' She took them off

him, burying her face in the brightly coloured petals. It was a delaying tactic, he realised sadly, because they gave off very little scent. Becky had no idea what to say to him so maybe he should put them both out of their misery.

'I'm sure you must have loads to do so I won't keep you. I just wanted to give you the flowers and wish you well. I hope you'll be very happy here, Becky. You deserve to be.'

'That's what Tom said.' There was a catch in her voice that tugged at his heartstrings but he had to be strong.

'Tom gave you a hand to move in, did he? Great.'

'He and Hannah were brilliant. I wouldn't have managed half as well without their help.'

'That's good to hear.' He managed another smile even though his heart felt as though it was dangling round his heels. He should have been here to help her. He would have been, too, if he'd stuck to his plan to be her friend and nothing more. It was too late for regrets, however, so he had to make the best of it. He gave a tiny shrug, the weight of his heart weighing him down like a lump of lead. 'Anyhow, as I said, I don't want to hold you up...'

'You aren't.'

Colour ran up her cheeks when she realised how vehement she had sounded and Ewan couldn't help being intrigued. It appeared that Becky wasn't as eager for him to leave as he'd thought. He raised a brow, leaving her to elucidate, which she did in a breathy tone that completely destroyed his resolve to behave sensibly. How could he walk away when it appeared she wanted him to stay and wanted it badly, too?

'Everything's sorted out, amazingly enough.' She gave a tinkly little laugh that wouldn't have convinced the least perceptive person that she hadn't a care in the world. It certainly didn't convince him. 'There's nothing left to do.'

'As you say, that's amazing,' Ewan agreed, wondering if he was misreading the signals. Maybe he had it all wrong and Becky wasn't really trying to find a reason to detain him?

'Would you like to come in and have a look?' She opened the door and his heart gave an almighty bounce as it reclaimed its rightful place in his chest when he saw the plea in her eyes. 'After all, you helped me find this place, Ewan, so it seems only right that you should see the finished result.'

'I'd love to. Thank you.'

Ewan stepped into the tiny hall, ignoring the taunting little voice in his head that seemed rather keen to remind him that he'd had very little to do with her decision to rent the cottage. The truth was all well and good, but sometimes it was better dispensed with! He followed her into the sitting room, and looked around in genuine amazement. There were pictures on the walls, knick-knacks on the coffee table and cushions piled invitingly on the sofa.

'Good lord! It looks as though you've been living here for ages. I wish my flat looked half as cosy as this does.'

'It's lovely, isn't it?' Becky agreed, looking around with satisfaction. 'I can't believe how well everything has come together.' She plumped up a purple silk cushion and placed it back on the sofa. 'I'm really thrilled.'

'No wonder. You've worked miracles to get it

all done in a day.' Ewan hesitated but he knew it had to be said. 'I'm sorry I wasn't here to help.'

'That's okay.' She gave a little shrug but he saw the hurt that crossed her face, and sighed.

'It isn't though, is it?' He touched her arm, felt the flash of awareness that arced through his body, and moved his hand away. 'I should have been here to help you, Becky.'

'Don't worry about it. I expect you were busy. Now, how about a cup of tea? I'm afraid I don't have anything stronger so I can't even offer you a glass of wine.'

'No, thank you.' Ewan felt frustration bubble up inside him. She seemed determined to gloss over his inadequacies and it wasn't right. Maybe she hadn't missed him but he had missed her!

He spun round on his heel, knowing that he was on a very slippery slope. For the past two, very long, weeks he had done his best to be sensible. Every time he'd been tempted to phone her, he had reminded himself of the reason why it would be the wrong thing to do. Until he had decided if he could cope with them having a purely sexual relationship, he had to stay away from her and that meant no phone calls, no visits, nothing that might influence him one way or the other.

It was too important that he get it right. Too dangerous if he made a mistake. He had to be sure of what he wanted, one hundred per cent certain. If there was even the tiniest margin of doubt then it could all go horribly wrong and he could find his life in tatters.

'Don't go.'

The words were softly spoken yet they stopped him in his tracks. Ewan felt tension grip him as he stood there, half in and half out of the door. There was a roaring in his ears that seemed to grow louder with every second and yet he heard each word with perfect clarity as Becky continued.

'Please stay, Ewan. It's what I want more than anything.'

'Why?' His own voice sounded remarkably level given the fact that her answer was mind-bogglingly important to him.

'Because I missed you. Because the past two weeks have been so empty without you.' She paused and he realised that he was holding his breath. 'Because I need you in my life even if it's not going to be forever.'

Pain ripped through him. Nothing could have been clearer than that, could it? He turned around slowly, his heart aching when he saw the strain on her face. If this was hard for him, it was no less hard for her. The thought cut through all the clouds of uncertainty that had curdled his thoughts. Becky might not need him forever but she needed him now.

Two steps and she was in his arms, that was all it took. Ewan held her against his heart and knew she could feel it racing. It didn't matter; nothing mattered apart from the fact that she needed him. He bent and kissed her, softly and with a tenderness that stemmed from his love for her. Maybe she only wanted the comfort of sex from him but he would make sure that their lovemaking was as perfect as it could possibly be. It would be his gift to her, hopefully something she would remember with pleasure in the years to come.

The thought of the future sent a chill through

him but he refused to allow it to spoil things. Lifting his hands, he cupped her face, tilting her head so that he could deepen the kiss, his tongue sliding into the warm sweetness of her mouth with an ease that made him shudder. Becky wanted him. She wanted his kisses, his caresses; she wanted him as her lover. It might not be all he wanted from her but it was enough.

He swung her up into his arms and carried her to the sofa, pushing aside the cushions as he laid her down. Her eyes were half-closed, their hazel depths darkened with passion, and he kissed her again with an urgency that made her tremble. Reaching up, she took his face between her hands.

'This is what I want, Ewan. I'm sure about that.'

She drew his head down, her mouth opening under his, and he responded immediately. As he plundered her lips, any doubts he still had melted away. This was what he wanted too. He was sure.

He ran his hands down her body, following the curve of her breasts, the dip of her waist, the swell of her hips. They had never reached this point in the past; all they had shared had been that single mind-blowing kiss, and it was doubly exciting to have been given the licence to explore the soft, lush curves of her body.

His hands found the buttons down the front of her checked shirt and he carefully worked them free then hesitated before he drew it apart, wanting to take his time and savour the moment. His breath caught as he parted the folds of cotton and drank in the beauty of her body. Her skin was lightly tanned where the sun had touched it, pearly white beneath the black lace of her bra. Ewan slid the straps of her bra down her arms and lifted her breasts free, his heart pounding when he felt their weight nestle into his palms. Her nipples were already standing proud and erect yet they peaked even more when he drew them into his mouth. Becky wanted him and her body was telling him that too.

The thought was just too much. Ewan groaned as he claimed her mouth once more and kissed her, hotly, urgently, and with a hunger he couldn't disguise, and she responded with equal ardour.

Grasping the hem of his T-shirt, she pulled it over his head, their mouths parting just long enough to complete the action. Ewan was trembling as he allowed his weight to settle over her. He could feel her warmth seeping into his skin, feel her softness moulding itself to his shape.

Although he had made love to other women, nothing had prepared him for how he felt right then with Becky in his arms. It felt like the very first time he had ever made love, he realised in awe. There was a freshness about it, a thrill of discovery that made every touch, each caress seem untried, untested. Making love to Becky was unlike anything he had experienced before.

The room was dark, the moon that had been shining through the window while they were making love now hidden behind a cloud. Becky lay curled up on her side, watching Ewan while he slept. Although she couldn't see his face clearly, every feature was etched on her mind. The thick curl of his lashes lying on his cheeks, the slope of his nose—slightly crooked thanks to a skirmish on the rugby field— and the long mobile curve of his mouth, a mouth that had kissed every inch of her body.

A shiver ran through her at the thought. Making love with Ewan tonight had been a revelation. She had never experienced anything like it before. She let her mind drift, recalling the heat of his skin burning into hers, the feel of his hands caressing her, the strength and power of his erection as he had entered her. Was it the fact that it had been such a long time since she had made love that had made it all seem so much more intense? She wasn't sure. All she knew was that she had never experienced the range and depth of emotions she had discovered tonight in Ewan's arms.

'Can I move or do you plan on lying there, watching me, for a bit longer?'

The laughter in his voice made her smile and she grinned at him. 'I'm not sure. Give me a couple more minutes to decide, will you?'

'No way!' Rolling over, he scooped her into his arms with a speed that made her gasp. His lips were hot when they found hers, hot and hungry, and Becky sighed with pleasure. It seemed that Ewan hadn't tired of her just yet.

They made love again and once again it was so wonderful that Becky could scarcely believe what was happening. How could the simple touch of his hand on her breast make her feel as though she was flying? How could a kiss fill her with such intense pleasure? By the time their bodies joined in the most intimate act of all, her senses were awash. The deliciously male scent of Ewan's skin filled her nostrils, the touch of his fingers dancing over the soft inner skin of her thigh made her shudder, whilst the salty taste of perspiration when she touched his neck with the tip of her tongue was an aphrodisiac in itself.

Opening her eyes, she watched the dark shadow of his body looming over her and felt safe, secure, protected, listened to him breathing and knew that no matter what happened in the future, she would never regret what was happening now. Ewan had given her back something that had been missing for far too long. He had made her feel like a woman again and she would always be grateful to him for that, would always love him. It seemed only fitting that he should be the one to restore her femininity.

They fell asleep soon afterwards, their limbs entwined, their bodies spooned together. When they awoke the next morning, they were still holding onto each other. Ewan smiled as he turned her round and dropped a kiss on the tip of her nose.

'I couldn't bear to let you go.'

'Me too, or should that be neither?' Becky murmured. Had he any idea how sexy he looked lying there with his chest bare and his hair all rumpled? she wondered. Probably. After all, she wasn't the first woman Ewan had slept with, was she?

The thought was like a douse of cold water. Becky bit her lip as she tossed back the quilt. It was stupid to feel possessive, stupid and self-ish too. She wanted Ewan to meet someone else, wanted him to have a wife and a family in time. She couldn't keep him to herself even if she wanted to because it wouldn't be right.

'What's the matter?'

He caught her hand and pulled her back down

onto the bed. Becky shook her head because there was no way that she could tell him how she felt. How would lead to why and she couldn't take that risk, wouldn't risk having him tell her that it didn't matter if she could never give him a child, that he wanted her anyway. It would be far too easy to believe him.

'Nothing. It's just time I got up. Dad will be here soon with the furniture for Millie's bedroom,' she explained, relieved to have a valid excuse.

'In that case, I'd better get up as well.' He tossed back the quilt and she gulped as she was treated to an unobstructed view of his naked body as he got out of the bed. 'I'll give your father a hand to get everything upstairs…unless you'd rather I left, of course,' he added as an afterthought.

'I…no, of course not. Dad will be glad of your help.'

'It doesn't bother you, then? I mean, it will be pretty clear that I've spent the night if I'm here at this time of the morning.'

'It's fine. Really.' She shrugged. 'As we've said

before, folk will believe what they choose to believe whatever we do.'

'Fair enough.' He gave her a quick grin and Becky told herself she had imagined the fleeting sadness in his eyes. 'Right, last one in the shower has to make breakfast!'

He headed for the door and after a moment's hesitation Becky ran after him. They reached the bathroom at the same time and had a playful tussle in the doorway before Ewan solved the problem of who was going first by carrying her inside. He deposited her in the shower stall and turned on the tap, ignoring her squeals as cold water rained down on her head. Stepping in beside her, he picked up the soap and smiled wickedly.

'Here's the deal. Obviously I won the challenge but I'm prepared to be generous. I'll make breakfast if I can scrub your back.'

Becky pouted. 'What about the dishes?'

He rolled his eyes. 'Talk about driving a hard bargain! Okay. I'll make breakfast *and* do the dishes. Deal?'

Becky held out her hand. 'Deal!'

Ewan caught hold of her hand and pulled her to him so that their bodies collided, wet skin sliding slickly against wet skin. His voice sounded more like a growl, rumbling beneath the gushing of the water. 'I'll get round to the back scrubbing in a moment.'

Becky sighed as he bent and kissed her. She closed her eyes, savouring the coolness of the water, such a contrast to the heat of Ewan's mouth. If only they could freeze time life would be perfect but it wasn't going to happen.

At some point in the not too distant future she had to call a halt, even though the thought filled her with dread. Having Ewan back in her life had made such a difference. He'd brought sunshine and laughter, warmth and fun plus a whole lot more, but they couldn't carry on like this. Not when it could mean him missing out on something as important as a family. He would only regret it and, worse still, probably end up blaming her, and she couldn't bear it if that happened.

Wrapping her arms around his neck, she kissed him back, aware of just how precious this time was. It could be weeks or even months but at some point they would have to part. And this time it would be forever.

CHAPTER FOURTEEN

'I DON'T KNOW what you're on but can I have some, please? Nobody should look as cheerful as you do after the day we've had!'

Ewan laughed as Cathy followed him into the staffroom. It was three weeks since that first night he and Becky had spent together and, quite frankly, it felt as though life couldn't get much better. They spent as much time as possible together and the amazing thing was that they seemed to be remarkably in accord. They enjoyed doing the same things, laughed at the same jokes, even watched the same television programmes—with one or two exceptions, he amended ruefully, recalling Becky's love of reality shows, which he loathed. It was little wonder that he breezed through even the busiest days without it getting him down.

'I'm not sure if it will work for you,' he told Cathy with a grin.

'Try me.' She rolled her eyes. 'I'm open to any suggestions, believe me. My feet are killing me, my back aches, and as for the rest—well, booking myself into the knacker's yard could be my best option!'

'Sounds a bit extreme.' Ewan grabbed his jacket out of the locker. He was meeting Becky in town as they were planning on having dinner together. Her mother had offered to mind Millie so she was also spending the night at his flat. His heart, as well as various other bits of his anatomy, leapt at the thought. It was little wonder that he sounded a little strained as he offered Cathy some friendly advice. 'Why don't you book some time off? A break would do you the world of good.'

'And when do you think I'll be able to get any time off?' Cathy snorted. 'We're another nurse down since Laura left, so that makes three vacancies we're carrying. It's overtime for me, not a holiday, which is why I want to know what you're on that makes you so cheerful. Come on, Ewan, spill the beans!'

Ewan looked over his shoulder as though making sure the coast was clear. He bent closer to Cathy and lowered his voice. 'Love.'

'Pardon?' Cathy reared back and stared at him.

Ewan grinned. 'You wanted to know why I'm feeling so cheerful—well, it's all down to love.'

'Ah, I see. Pity. I thought it'd be something more prosaic, like some new drug you're testing or a super-duper new drink guaranteed to give you a boost.' She shook her head. 'Much as I love my husband, the days when the thought of seeing him put wings on my feet are long gone!'

Cathy took her bag out of the locker and left. Ewan chuckled as he followed her along the corridor. Maybe love did become less exciting with time but he couldn't imagine it, not if his feelings for Becky were anything to go by. As far as he was concerned, he would still find her exciting and sexy when they were both ninety!

The thought struck a chord, one he didn't want to think about. He headed into town, trying to ignore the tiny inner voice that was doing its best to have its say. So what if Becky hadn't said anything to indicate that she had changed her mind about them having a purely temporary relationship? He hadn't said anything either so he could hardly read anything into it. No, Becky needed to be sure about what she was doing after what had happened to her and he understood that. He was prepared to wait, however long it took.

She was already waiting outside the restaurant when he arrived. Ewan didn't hesitate as he took her in his arms. He would never get tired of kissing her, he thought, never, ever become complacent about their relationship. He had lost her once before and he was going to do his utmost not to lose her again.

'Hi,' he said softly as he reluctantly let her go. His gaze skimmed over her, drinking in the picture she made. She'd opted for cream trousers that night made from some sort of silky fabric that just hinted at the curves beneath. With them she was wearing a sleeveless top in a deep honey colour that made her hazel eyes look more gold than green and set off the light tan of her skin. She looked so beautiful that he felt his breath catch. He loved her so much and tonight he intended to tell her that too.

'Hi, yourself.' She laughed up at him, her nose wrinkling adorably. 'Do I take it from that very enthusiastic greeting that you missed me?'

'I did indeed.' Ewan grinned wickedly as he put his arm around her. 'I'd be more than happy to show you just how much, too. Why don't we skip dinner and go straight back to the flat?'

'No way!' She scooted out of his grasp and smiled up at him. 'I'm absolutely starving, so unless you want to risk me passing out, I need to eat.'

Ewan didn't try to change her mind. Opening the restaurant's door, he ushered her inside. A couple of times he'd sensed that she'd been pulling back, but he understood. Becky didn't want them to go too fast. Neither did he really, only sometimes—like now—it was hard to remember that. He took a deep breath as he followed her inside. He had to be patient, give her time to adjust to the idea of them being together. If he pushed her he could end up losing her and that was the last thing he wanted.

* * *

The evening was perfect, but it always was when she was with Ewan. Becky spooned up the last of her raspberry mousse, determined not to let anything spoil the evening. She knew it couldn't last and that at some point they would have to break up, but not tonight. Tonight she was going to be with Ewan.

The thought sent heat flowing through her veins and she picked up her glass and took a sip of the wine. Their lovemaking had continued to be incredible. Although it seemed impossible, each time they made love it simply got better. She'd read that phrase about two people becoming one and dismissed it; now she knew it could and did happen. She couldn't imagine how she was going to feel when Ewan was no longer part of her life.

'That was delicious.' Putting down her glass, she smiled at him, refusing to go down that path. It was the here and now that mattered, not what happened in the future. 'How did you find this place? You never said.'

'One of the nurses recommended it.' Ewan sat

back in his chair and groaned. 'I am *so* full I think I might burst!'

'Oh, I see. She's got good taste, obviously,' Becky replied, trying to keep the edge out of her voice. Feeling jealous at the thought of the nurse recommending the restaurant to him was ridiculous. Ewan was free to talk to whomever he liked.

'He.' He smiled but there was a glint in his eyes that told her he'd picked up on her feelings. 'It was Rob who recommended the place to me. He's one of the charge nurses on the unit and a great guy too.'

'My mistake.' Becky attempted to brush it off but Ewan wasn't prepared to let it go.

'I'm not seeing anyone else, Becky, firstly because I don't want to and secondly because it wouldn't be right when I'm seeing you.'

'I didn't meant to imply that you were,' she said shortly, and he sighed.

'Maybe not, but you're bound to have doubts after what Steve did.' He shrugged. 'I know I had a reputation for playing the field in the past and that it was probably justified too. But I'm strictly a one-woman-at-a-time kind of a guy.'

'I know.' Becky smiled, putting every scrap of effort into making it appear genuine; however, his reassurances had done little to comfort her. Ewan might not choose to date more than one woman at a time but he hadn't claimed that he'd be eternally faithful to her, had he?

As that was the last thing she wanted, Becky realised how ridiculous she was being. She put it out of her mind as Ewan paid the bill. They walked back to his flat hand in hand because they both needed the contact. Ewan let them in, then took her in his arms as he kicked the door shut.

'Got you to myself at last,' he growled in a tone that was meant to be humorous but some-how fell short of the mark.

Becky closed her eyes as he kissed her, letting herself be carried away by the feel of his mouth and the promise of his touch. He was as eager for her as she was for him and that was all that mattered. As he led her into his bedroom, she knew that no matter what happened in the future, she would always have this. Ewan made her feel whole again, complete. Nobody else could have done this, only him. He made her feel like a real woman and she loved him all the more because of it.

Their lovemaking seemed to reach new heights that night, as though they both needed to prove to themselves as well as to each other how deep their feelings were. As Becky lay in his arms later, she knew that nothing could ever be as profound as what they had just shared. If this wasn't love then what was? The thought filled her with dread. She couldn't allow Ewan to fall in love with her!

'I love you.'

The words were so softly spoken that for a moment Becky thought they had escaped from her head, but then she realised that Ewan was looking at her and her heart seemed to freeze.

'No. Please don't say that.'

'Why not when it's true?' He brushed her mouth with his knuckles and a spasm passed through her, compounded partly of fear and partly of desire. 'I love you, Becky, and not saying it won't change how I feel.'

'I don't want you to love me, though!' The words slid out before she could stop them and she saw him wince.

'Because you still love Steve?' He shrugged, deliberately trying to downplay the hurt she could see in his eyes. 'I understand, Becky. Really I do.'

Becky knew that she could leave it there, that he would accept it and not push her, but it seemed wrong to let him believe a lie. 'It isn't that.'

'No? Then what is it?' He laid his hand against her cheek. 'Tell me, sweetheart. I don't want there to be any secrets between us even if the truth is far more painful.'

'I…' She stopped, afraid to go on yet unable to mislead him. She loved him too but that wasn't the issue. It was bigger than that, far, far bigger. She took a steadying breath. 'One day you'll want to have a family, won't you, Ewan?'

His hand lowered as he stared at her in confusion. 'Probably, yes. But what's that got to do with it?' He paused for a moment then said slowly, 'Are you saying that you don't want any more children, Becky?'

Becky knew she could use that as her excuse but it would be wrong. Ewan deserved the truth, nothing less. 'No. I would love to have more children but it isn't possible. I had a hysterectomy following the accident. The fact is that I can't have any more children—now do you understand?'

He did. He understood perfectly. All of a sudden Ewan couldn't speak, couldn't move, could barely breathe as the enormity of what she'd said hit him: Becky couldn't have any more children. She could never have *his* child.

'I'm so sorry, Ewan. This is exactly what I was trying to avoid. I never wanted to hurt you.'

Tears clogged her voice and the feeling came rushing back to his limbs. Reaching out, he pulled her into his arms, praying that he could find a way to comfort her. If he was hurting, how much worse must it be for her? 'It's all right, my love. Don't cry. It isn't your fault. None of it is your fault.'

His voice broke at that point, the tears he'd

been struggling to hold back streaming down his face, and it was her turn to offer comfort. Wrapping her arms around him, she held him to her and he could feel her love pouring out of her and into him. It was almost too painful to realise how much she loved him at this most desperately sad moment.

They clung to one another for a long time before Ewan gently set her away from him. Although it was a blow to discover that they could never have a child, it didn't change how he felt about her. He loved her with all his heart, needed her in his life, couldn't imagine a future without her. Now all he had to do was convince her that their relationship could work.

'I wish it could have been different, Becky, really I do, but it doesn't alter how I feel about you. I love you and the fact that we can't have a family doesn't change anything.'

'Maybe not at the moment it doesn't but it could do in the future.' Her tone was bleak. 'The time will come when you realise just how much you are missing by not having a family of your own. I know how fond you are of your nephews and nieces and it's only natural that you'd want a child of your own one day. I can never give you a child, Ewan, and I couldn't bear it if you ended up hating me for denying you something so important.'

'I could never hate you!' He went to take her in his arms again, appalled that she could think such a thing, but she pushed him away.

'You don't know how you'll feel in a few years' time and it's a risk I'm not prepared to take.'

'So you think it's better that we split up?' he said harshly, scarcely able to believe what was happening. To plummet from the heights of euphoria to the depths of despair in mere minutes was just too much to take in.

'Yes, I do. I won't be responsible for ruining your life, Ewan.'

'You could never do that.' He captured her hands and held them tightly, willing her to understand that he meant every word. 'I need you, Becky. I know we can be happy even if we can't have a child together. We'll have Millie, don't forget, and she's such a joy.'

'She is but she isn't your flesh and blood, Ewan.'

'I don't care about that—really I don't!' He gripped her hands harder, desperate to convince her. 'I love her and I can't think of anything I'd like more than to be a proper father to her.'

'And you'd be a wonderful father too. I know that, Ewan, but it doesn't change how I feel. It wouldn't be fair to allow you to sacrifice your chances of having a child of your own for me and Millie.'

She gently freed herself and tossed back the quilt. Ewan lay quite still, his head reeling, his heart in turmoil. He could try again to change her mind but he knew it would be a waste of time. Becky had made her decision and nothing he said would change it.

Despair washed over him in a huge grey tide. He couldn't bear to imagine how empty his life was going to be without her. When Becky came back and climbed into bed beside him, he drew her into his arms, drinking in the scent of her skin, the warmth of her body, the very essence of her being.

'I love you, Becky. Always remember that,' he said, his voice grating.

'And I love you too.'

The words should have been the sweetest in the world but they filled him with pain. Ewan closed his eyes, praying that sleep would offer some relief from the agony, although he knew it would be only temporary. Nothing was going to change. Tomorrow he would have to learn to live without her and he wasn't sure if he could do it.

It was raining when Becky got up the next morning. Surprisingly, she had slept heavily, her mind too filled with pain to dream. She made coffee and took a mug through to the bedroom for Ewan. He was wide awake, staring at the ceiling, and she didn't need to ask what he was thinking. It was obvious from his expression how devastated he felt.

'Don't.' She put the mug on the bedside table and sat down on the edge of the bed. 'I don't want you torturing yourself, Ewan. You have to accept that you and I are going nowhere and get on with your life. It's as simple as that.'

'Is it?' His smile was forced. 'Then why do I feel like this? If it's so simple, I should know that you've made the right decision.'

'It's been a shock. Once you're thinking clearly, you'll see that it would be a mistake if we got back together properly.'

'Properly? So the last few weeks don't really count?' His laughter was harsh and she flinched. 'Thanks a bunch, sweetheart. You really know how to cheer a guy up.'

'I didn't say that. Of course they count. They've been wonderful, the most wonderful time of my life, in fact.' She shook her head when he went to speak. 'But that was before we faced the facts and the fact is that if we stay together, we can't have a family. I can't give you a child, Ewan. Not ever.'

She stood up, unable to go over it all again. Picking up her clothes, she went into the bathroom and took a shower, trying not to think about the times Ewan had joined her there. There was no point thinking about what had happened and certainly no point thinking about what might have been. Their relationship had to end. And she had to make sure it did, no matter what Ewan said.

He was in the kitchen when she went to find him. He looked round and her heart ached when she saw the anguish in his eyes. He was hurting badly and what made it worse was knowing that she was responsible.

'I have to go. I'm sorry about what's happened but I hope we can still be friends.'

'So we can meet up for coffee?' He shrugged. 'I can't see that happening, Becky, can you? It's probably best if we make a clean break.'

'If that's what you want,' she said, wondering how she could bear the thought of not seeing him again.

'It isn't what I want. It's what you want, apparently.'

Tears stung her eyes when she heard the censure in his voice. 'I'm simply doing what I believe is right, Ewan. If you're honest then you know it would be madness to carry on. You'd end up hating me for not being able to give you a child and that isn't what either of us wants.'

She turned away before he could reply, afraid

that if she didn't leave then, she wouldn't find the strength to do so. Ewan didn't try to stop her as she let herself out and that in itself seemed to prove her point. In his heart, he knew she was right, knew that no matter how much they loved one another, their relationship was doomed.

It was barely seven when she let herself into the cottage. She changed into her uniform then drove to the surgery. Hannah had just arrived as well and she grinned when she saw Becky.

'Another early bird. Charlie had us up at five so that's my explanation for such an early arrival. What's yours?'

'Oh, I woke up early too,' Becky said shortly, feeling her eyes fill with foolish tears once more.

'Hey, what's up? Have you and Ewan had a row?' Hannah grimaced when Becky looked at her. 'Ros happened to mention that you were staying over at his flat last night. Sorry. I didn't mean to pry.'

'That's okay.' Becky tried to smile but her mouth wouldn't seem to obey her.

'Come along.' Hannah took her arm and steered her through the surgery doors, quickly dispensing with the alarm before it started ringing. 'I think a cup of tea is called for, don't you?'

Hannah briskly led her to the staffroom, ignoring her protests that she was fine. Becky sank down on a chair while Hannah made the tea, wondering what she was going to do. There weren't that many options. She and Ewan had to go their separate ways, so she would just have to learn to live without him. Tears streamed down her cheeks and Hannah pressed a cup of tea into her hands.

'Here you are. Drink this and tell me all about it.'

Becky did as she was told, letting the whole sorry story come tumbling out. Hannah sighed when she had finished. 'Oh, Becky, I don't know what to say. It's so awful for both of you. Are you sure that you and Ewan can't find a way around the problem? I mean, you could adopt or even try to find a surrogate. It's perfectly acceptable these days.'

'But why should Ewan have to go through all that to have children? There's nothing wrong with him. It's me who can't give him a child.'

She shook her head. 'No. He needs to find some-one else, someone who can give him a family.'

'And who's to say that if he does find someone else, she can have kids? Or even if Ewan himself can have them? I mean, nobody really knows if they can until they try. Imagine how you'd both feel if that happened.'

'Don't!' Becky shivered. 'The only thing that's keeping me going is the thought of Ewan being a father one day. I can't bear to imagine it all going wrong.'

'I'm sorry. I don't mean to upset you, but you need to think about this. You love Ewan and he loves you. That's an awful lot to give up for something that might never happen anyway. Plus there's Millie. Anyone can see that Ewan thinks the world of her. Maybe she isn't his biological child but Ewan loves her just as Tom loves my Charlie.'

Hannah gave her an encouraging smile before she left the staffroom. Becky finished her tea, wondering if Hannah was right. Was it wrong to give up their love for something that wasn't a guaranteed certainty?

She sighed. She was looking for reasons for her and Ewan to stay together because she loved him so much. However, at the end of the day, she knew it wouldn't be fair to let him make such a huge sacrifice. She had to let him go no matter how much it hurt.

CHAPTER FIFTEEN

A WEEK PASSED, the longest, most agonising week of Ewan's life. Although he had been upset when Becky had left him eight years ago, it had been nothing to compared to this. Fortunately, life in ED continued to be hectic so everyone was far too busy to notice his downbeat mood, even the ever-perceptive Cathy. Ewan knew that he couldn't have explained what was wrong. It was far too painful to talk about why his heart was broken.

Saturday night arrived and he volunteered to work overtime when the agency registrar failed to turn up. Rob Blessing, the senior charge nurse who'd recommended that restaurant he'd visited with Becky that fateful night, was on duty. He grinned when he saw Ewan making his way to the desk.

'Here comes the cavalry.' He peered past

Ewan, a look of mock surprise on his face. Rob was happily gay and very involved in amateur dramatics. 'Don't tell me you're riding solo tonight, cowboy.'

'Yep. There's just me and my trusty steed, only I think he's deserted me too and gone back to his stable.' Ewan made a determined effort and smiled. 'It's just you and me, pardner. Think we can handle it?'

'No sweat! We'll soon sort out the bad guys.'

The phone rang at that point so Rob passed him a file and answered it. Ewan made his way to the cubicles. His patient was a child, a boy aged ten who had come off his bike and injured his arm. His mother was with him and Ewan had to spend a few minutes calming her down before he could examine the boy.

'Right, then, Ethan, let's see what damage you've done to yourself.'

He carefully removed the sling the paramedics had used to support the boy's arm and discovered that his shoulder was dislocated. It was a forward and downward displacement, typical of a fall onto an outstretched hand.

'Hmm, looks like you've popped your shoulder out of its socket,' he told the boy in a deliberately upbeat tone that was at odds with his mood. Could he live out the rest of his life without Becky? Could he see himself growing old with someone else, because that's what it would mean? If he didn't find someone else and have a family then it would make a mockery of their sacrifice, yet he couldn't imagine it happening. How could he make love to another woman when it was Becky he loved, Becky he wanted, Becky he needed?

'I told you something like this would happen!' Ethan's mother's voice was shrill as she rounded on her son. Ewan hurriedly collected his thoughts.

'It's a fairly common injury,' he said soothingly. 'All it takes is a fall and—bingo—out it pops. We'll soon get it sorted out, so don't worry that Ethan's done himself any permanent damage. Give it a couple of weeks and his shoulder will be as good as new.'

'It should never have happened in the first place,' Mrs Jones declared. 'I told him he wasn't to go on that new BMX track but he took no notice.' She turned to the boy. 'Well, it's the last time this is going to happen, my lad. As soon as we get home, I'm going to put your bike up for sale!'

Ethan started to cry and Ewan frowned. The child had been extremely brave and it didn't seem fair that he should be treated so harshly. 'That seems a little harsh, if you don't mind my saying so. Your son could have popped his shoulder if he'd tripped over in the street.'

'But he didn't, did he? He came off his bike and it's not going to happen again.' Mrs Jones glared at him. 'It's obvious that you don't have any kids, Doctor, but when you do, you'll realise that you can't give them an inch or you'll regret it.'

Ewan forbore saying anything, afraid that anything he said would be unprofessional. He wrote out an instruction for the boy's shoulder and arm to be X-rayed as a fall like this often caused damage to the humerus and left the cubicle. If he and Becky got married then he would never get the chance to be a father, except to Millie, of course. Would he come to feel that he had missed out, as Becky believed, or would it be enough that he had her and Millie to love and care for? Pictures suddenly flashed through his head, pictures of the fun he'd had playing with Millie that day at the beach. He wouldn't have enjoyed it any more if Millie had been his *biological* daughter.

The thought was a much-needed boost to his spirits. As he made his way to the desk, he decided that he wasn't going to give up. Somehow he had to make Becky see that they could be happy together despite everything. He obviously looked more cheerful because Rob grimaced when he saw him.

'You aren't going to look nearly as happy when you hear what I have to tell you.'

'Why? What's happened?'

'It seems there's been a fight at one of the caravan parks. A gang of youths have knocked seven bells out of each other.' Rob sighed. 'The police are ferrying them in so we can patch them up.'

'Great.' Ewan glanced at the queue of people waiting to be seen. 'Looks like there's going to be a bit of a backlog. Any chance of drafting in some reinforcements to help?'

'What do you think?' Rob replied tartly.

The first police van arrived just then so Ewan went out to meet it. There were three young men inside, not much more than teenagers really, and they all had cuts and bruises.

'Right, you lot,' he said, knowing that they needed to know who was in charge. 'I shall make this clear: anyone who doesn't behave himself won't be treated. So no swearing at the staff and no causing a nuisance to the other patients. You're to sit quietly until your name is called. Understand?'

There was a bit of muttering but no real objections. Ewan led them inside and sat them down. The police had to go back to collect some more of the wounded but they left an officer behind to keep an eye on things. Ewan took the first youth into a cubicle, using glue to close the cut over his eye before he sent him on his way. If the police wanted to interview him, they would have to take him to the station. He was more concerned about clearing the decks before the next influx.

They worked as a team. He and Rob dealt with the worst cases while Moira and Trish saw to the rest. In a very short time most of the youths had been seen. Rob nodded towards the waiting room, which was packed.

'I'll see to the last of this little lot if you'll make a start on the rest.'

'Will do.' Ewan picked up the next patient's notes. 'Amanda Lewis. Can you follow me, please?'

He led the woman into a cubicle. She'd twisted her ankle and as it looked very swollen he decided to send her for an X-ray to make sure it wasn't broken. Rob was in the next cubicle and he could hear voices being raised as he wrote out the slip and handed it to her. 'Along the corridor on your right. Just knock on the door and someone will come out to you. Do you need a wheelchair?'

'No, my boyfriend can help me,' Amanda told him. She grimaced when there was a crash from next door. 'I'll be glad to get away from here.'

Ewan hurried out of the cubicle and into the neighbouring one, taking in the scene that greeted him. Rob was trying to calm down his patient, who had overturned the trolley containing supplies. 'Everything okay in here?' he asked, neutrally.

'Fine.' Rob grinned. 'Jez here isn't too keen on having an injection, it appears. We had a difference of opinion, shall we say?'

'Too right we did.' The teenager rounded on Ewan, his face contorted into an ugly expression. 'I'm not having the likes of him putting needles in me. I might catch something!'

It was a direct reference to Rob's sexuality and Ewan couldn't let it pass. 'You were warned that if you didn't behave yourself you wouldn't be treated. I think you'd better leave.' He flipped back the curtain and waited but the youth didn't move. 'The police are outside. Do you really want me to call them in? You're in enough trouble as it is.'

Jez glowered at him. 'Do what you like but he's not putting his hands on me.'

Ewan had heard quite enough. Stepping forward, he took hold of the boy's arm. 'Come on, don't make this worse for yourself than it already is.'

He went to lead him towards the corridor, stopping when he felt something punch him hard in the chest. He looked down in surprise when he saw a knife sticking out of his body. Where had that come from? he wondered before everything started to go dark. There was a rushing in his head, the feeling that he was falling, down and down, and then nothing.

Becky was in her room when Tom came to find her. It was Monday morning and she'd just done a BP check on one of his patients and assumed he was eager for the results.

'You were right, her BP is rather low,' she told him, picking up the notes. 'One hundred over fifty so it will need checking again.'

'Thanks. I'll get Lizzie to make another appointment for her.' Tom paused as though he wasn't sure what to say next and Becky laughed.

'Come on, spit it out. If you want me to fit

someone else into my list then I promise not to bite your head off.'

'It's not that.' He took a deep breath. 'I've just been speaking to a friend of mine at Pinscombe General. He told me that Ewan's on the cardiac unit.'

'Is he? How odd. He loves working in ED so I wonder why he's changed specialities?' Becky tried to keep her tone even, although after a week of not seeing Ewan it was hard to hold back her tears. She missed him so much and couldn't bear to imagine a future without him, even though she knew it was the right thing to do.

'He hasn't. He's a patient.' Tom's tone was gentle. 'It appears he was stabbed on Saturday night. The knife went straight into his heart.'

'Stabbed!' Becky exclaimed in horror.

'Yes.' Tom came around the desk and sat her down. 'It's bad, Becky. You need to know that, but he is alive.' He squeezed her hands. 'Hannah told me about you two splitting up because you can't have children, but I thought you'd want to know.'

'Of course.' Becky took a deep breath, trying

desperately to clear her head. Ewan was hurt and she needed to be with him; nothing else mattered except that. She jumped up and grabbed her bag out of the drawer. 'Can you tell Lizzie that I have to go out? I don't know what she's going to do about my appointments…'

'We'll work something out,' Tom assured her. He followed her into the corridor. 'Are you sure you're fit to drive? I can phone for a taxi if you want.'

'No. I just need to get to the hospital and see Ewan.'

'Of course. Give him our love, won't you?' Tom told her and she nodded, afraid to admit how scared she was that it might not be possible. If Ewan died she wouldn't be able to give him her colleagues' love or her own.

Tears blurred her eyes as she hurried out to her car but she blinked them away. It seemed to take forever to get to the hospital and then there was all the hassle of finding a parking space. In the end she parked on double yellow lines. The car wasn't in the way and she didn't care if she got a ticket. It took her another few minutes to find the cardio unit and when she arrived, she was told that Ewan had been moved to ICU. His condition had worsened in the last hour and it had been decided that he needed specialised nursing care.

Becky could barely contain her anguish as she made her way to ICU and went through the rigmarole of explaining who she was. Fortunately, Ewan's parents were there and they vouched for her but it all took time. Then she had to wait while the consultant finished examining him but finally she was allowed in to see him.

She made her way to the bed, trying to ignore all the tubes and monitors he was attached to. She knew they were essential but it was a shock to see him like this, so still, so pale, so very vulnerable. Ewan had always been very fit, always been strong in mind as well as body, and it hurt to see him lying there like that. Sitting down beside the bed, she covered his hand with hers, mindful of the wires leading from it.

'Ewan, it's me, Becky. I'm sorry I didn't come sooner. I didn't know what had happened, you see, but I'm here now and I'm going to stay until you're better. I love you so much, my darling. You have to try really hard to fight this because I need you.'

A sob welled to her throat and she stopped, not wanting him to hear her crying. He couldn't die. Not when she needed him so much. Maybe she couldn't give him a family but she could love him with all her heart and that had to count for a lot.

'I love you,' she repeated. 'I love you so much, Ewan. Please don't leave me.'

Consciousness came back in a rush. One minute there was nothing but blankness and the next he could feel and hear. Someone was talking to him, a voice he recognised, although for a second he couldn't place it. And then he realised it was Becky and sighed. Everything would be all right now that Becky was here.

He turned towards her, forcing his eyelids to open, but they wouldn't move. He tried again but they seemed to be stuck together… He flinched when the tape was removed, taking one of his eyelashes with it. However, at least he could see and that was a relief. His gaze rested on her as a rush of emotions hit him. He loved her so much, far too much to let her go. Maybe they could never have a family but they could have each other and that was more than enough. He would devote his life to loving her and Millie, and be happy.

'Ewan, can you hear me?' She bent over him, her hazel eyes filled with worry, and his heart wept for what he must have put her through.

'Yes,' he whispered because his throat was raw from having had a tube down it. Unlike all those scenes in the movies when the unconscious patient awoke and had no idea what had happened, he remembered everything: the pain in his chest, the darkness, followed by nothing....

He shuddered, not wanting to think about that. He was alive and Becky was here with him—that was all that mattered. 'I love you,' he said hoarsely, praying that she understood what he was trying to say.

Her face lit up so it appeared that she did. 'I love you too, so very much.' She kissed him with exquisite gentleness and he groaned in frustration. He didn't want kid-glove treatment—he wanted passion!

'Did I hurt you?' The anxiety in her voice made him smile because it was so totally misplaced.

'Nope. I'd just prefer it if you kissed me with a bit more enthusiasm, shall we say?'

She chuckled as she glanced over her shoulder. 'I shall once we dispense with our audience.'

Ewan peered past her and only then realised that his parents were standing outside the glass wall of the cubicle. That they had heard what he'd said was only too apparent from the expression on his mother's face. Ewan bit back a chuckle as he promised himself that when Millie grew up, he would accept that she was an adult and had needs.

The fact that he was picturing himself playing a major role in Millie's future suddenly filled him with doubts. What if Becky didn't agree? What if she still insisted that they had to split up? He had to make her understand how wrong it would be. He needed her. She needed him. And they both needed Millie.

'I don't want us to part, Becky,' he said urgently. 'I understand why you think it's the right thing to do but I can't bear it.'

'I don't want it either, so long as you're sure, Ewan.' She looked into his eyes, searching for the truth, and smiled when she found it. 'Thank you. That you're willing to give up so much for me makes me realise how lucky I am.'

'I'm the lucky one. I get to have you and Millie in my life long term.' He smiled back, unashamed of the tears in his eyes. 'I love you both. You're my heart, my soul and my family.'

They kissed then, not the light touch of lips their audience expected but a kiss of passion and commitment, of promise and desire. Ewan felt Becky's lips on his and could feel the strength flowing back into his body. Becky had done this. She had given him the best reason in the world to get better. She had promised him herself and her love, and her daughter. He had to be the luckiest man alive.

Two years later...

'It's a boy! Here you go, mum. Meet your new son.'

Becky felt her heart overflow with happiness

as she took the towel-wrapped bundle from the midwife. She stared down at the tiny, puckered face in wonder. The baby had Ewan's nose and his eyes. His hair was dark like Ewan's too and she knew it would stay that way. This little chap was going to be the image of his father when he grew up.

'I can't believe how much he looks like you.' Ewan gently parted the folds of towel and stared at his son in amazement. 'He's the image of you, Becky!'

Becky laughed. 'I was just thinking how much he favoured you. Look at his eyes and the shape of his nose. If that's not a MacLeod nose, I don't know what is!'

'I see we shall have to agree to differ.' Ewan hugged her. 'Well, whomever he favours, he's gorgeous and I can't wait to show him off to everyone.'

'Neither can I. I just want to thank Shona again for all she's done.'

'Me too.'

They went over to the bed. All three of Ewan's sisters had offered to act as a surrogate for them but in the end Shona had won. She and her family had moved back to Devon, so that had made the process a lot simpler. Becky's eggs had been fertilised by Ewan's sperm and Shona had, as she put it, acted as the incubator. Amazingly, it had taken just one attempt for her to get pregnant and they were holding the result in their arms. Becky bent and kissed her sister-in-law on the cheek.

'Thank you from the very bottom of my heart. I can't tell you what this means to us.'

'I think I can guess.' Shona smiled as she held her husband's hand tightly. He'd been behind her every step of the way, which had made it feel even more right. 'Now go and show off your new son to his adoring fans. There'll be a riot out there if they don't get a glimpse of him soon!'

Becky laughed as she followed Ewan to the delivery room door. They were all there, waiting to meet the new arrival: her family, her mother holding tight to Millie's hand; her father and brother, both looking uncharacteristically anxious; Ewan's family, complete with various nieces and nephews. Tom and Hannah had brought along the latest addition to their family, six-week-old Olivia, as well as Charlie, while Ben, Emily and Theo had flown over from France especially for this moment. Turning so that they could all see the precious little bundle she held, Becky said the words she had never thought she would be able to say.

'We would like you all to meet James Ewan MacLeod. Our son.'

* * * * *

Mills & Boon® Large Print
Medical

February

March

April

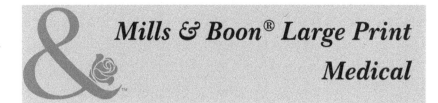

Mills & Boon® Large Print Medical

May

June

July

0114 LP 2P P2 Medical